VANISHING WORLD

Also by Sayaka Murata

Life Ceremony

Earthlings

Convenience Store Woman

VANISHING WORLD

A NOVEL

SAYAKA MURATA

TRANSLATED FROM THE JAPANESE
BY GINNY TAPLEY TAKEMORI

Grove Press
New York

Originally published as *Shōmetsu sekai*. Original Japanese edition published by Kawade Shobo Shinsha, Ltd., Tokyo. English language translation rights reserved to Grove Atlantic, Inc. under license granted by Sayaka Murata through Aragi, Inc.

Published simultaneously in Canada
Printed in the United States of America

First Grove Atlantic hardcover edition: April 2025

Library of Congress Cataloging-in-Publication data is available for this title.

ISBN 978-0-8021-6466-7
eISBN 978-0-8021-6467-4

Grove Press
an imprint of Grove Atlantic
154 West 14th Street
New York, NY 10011

Distributed by Publishers Group West

groveatlantic.com

25 26 27 28 10 9 8 7 6 5 4 3 2 1

VANISHING WORLD

"Aren't we kind of the opposite of Adam and Eve?" a boyfriend once asked me, long ago.

I was twenty years old and had taken this boyfriend home at a time when I knew nobody would be in.

I had been dozing off in sheets that were infused with our body heat and opened my eyes a crack as this curious question came fluttering down along with the sound of the rain outside.

"What do you mean, the opposite?"

"Well, look, Adam and Eve ate the forbidden fruit and were banished from paradise, right? Like, they were the first man and woman ever to have sex. So supposing humans were headed back to paradise and there was a last couple to ever have sex, they'd be the opposite of Adam and Eve, wouldn't they?"

"Is that what happened?" I responded sleepily. "There I was thinking that Adam ate the fruit of good and evil and then had to go out to work to get food to eat, while Eve was made to suffer even worse pain in childbirth. Or something like that."

"Oh, really?" he said, and lit up a cigarette. "But then, don't we only know about pleasure and shame because Adam ate the fruit? I've always had this image of you being the last Eve, Amane. I mean, while everyone else is returning to paradise, you're the last human left having sex."

"What the hell? That's creepy! It sounds like a curse."

"Well anyway, that's how it feels to me." He stroked my hair.

"No way!"

I laughed, but it felt like a curse had seeped into my body and stuck under my skin and wouldn't go away.

Dawn that morning was accompanied by the sound of heavy rain, just like the day I was born.

PART ONE

Until I went to elementary school, I lived entirely in a world my mother had created.

I did go to daycare, but I don't remember much about it. What comes to mind when I think back to that time is the small old wooden house in Chiba where I lived with my mother, just the two of us.

My parents had divorced and my father had already left home by the time I was in daycare, but there were photos of him all over the house—on the TV stand, on my mother's vanity, everywhere. My mother would open up an album stuffed with photos of him holding me as a baby and tell me over and over, "Daddy loved you, you know, Amane."

The house had been left to us by my grandmother when she died. From outside it looked like a typical Japanese house, but inside it was decorated in a Western style, with red carpet throughout, darkened with age.

Red was my mother's favorite color. There was a small red sofa in the living room, and the curtains were patterned with red flowers. When night fell, a small glass lamp emitted a dim red light. The interior was tastelessly mismatched, with an old paper shoji behind the red sofa, but my mother would always say, "Red is the color of love, that's why I like it."

My mother put a bed in the small upstairs tatami room, and she slept in that while I slept on a futon spread out on the floor beside it. She liked to tell me about how she and my father had first met, and it always sounded like something out of a fairytale.

"Mummy and Daddy loved each other very much, Amane. And it's because we fell in love, got married, and lived happily together that you were born."

"Uh huh," I said obediently.

She would turn the pages of the album like it was a picture book. The tall, timid-looking young man with an earnest face in the photos was my father, she told me. I didn't feel any connection to him, but in this house with just the two of us, what she said was absolute.

"We as good as eloped, you know. We really, really loved each other."

"Yes."

"When you grow up, Amane, you too will marry the man you love and have his baby. It'll be such a cute child."

In addition to that album, the house was full of dog-eared old picture books that contained tales about princes and princesses falling in love and living happily ever after. I wanted nice new books like we had in daycare, but I was always flatly rejected when I begged for these.

"Amane, you too will one day fall in love, get married, and have children, just like Mummy and Daddy. And the two of you will live happily bringing up your precious children. Do you understand?"

"Uh huh."

She was always in a good mood when I listened to her meekly. I didn't like daycare much, and my mother's world was everything to me.

And so I grew up absorbing into my body the "right" world, as provided by my mother.

As I started nodding off, the warmth of my mother's body, the sensation of her soft breast pushing against my cheek, and her monotone whisper all grew slowly more distant. Through my closed eyelids, I could sense the light from the red lamp she had placed on the floor. I always felt as though I was being sucked into that red light as I fell asleep.

The first time I fell in love was with a boy I saw on TV, back when I was still going to daycare.

In any romance, there is always a specific moment when you fall in love. Until that moment, I had simply found the program entertaining enough that I made a point of turning on the TV to watch it every week because so many of the other children in daycare liked it.

It was a popular animation series, and every Thursday evening I was glued to the TV like all the other children my age.

The story was about a seven-thousand-year-old immortal boy who little by little restored colors to the world after they had been stolen from it.

To begin with, I thought the show was weird, as the screen started off completely dark, and you could only hear a voice.

Eventually, though, Lapis restored "white," and the screen became black and white. That's when I saw his face for the first time. He had sharp, catlike eyes and the appearance of a fourteen-year-old boy.

As the story progressed, Lapis restored all the colors to the world one by one. Yellow, purple, green . . . and when he restored red, I was shocked to see blood coming from his body.

Then blue was restored, and the sky and sea all at once took on color. And I couldn't stop crying after the scene in which Lapis's eyes finally turned blue.

Even after losing an arm and a leg, Lapis kept battling to save the show's heroine. When he still kept fighting even after his face was cut and he had only one finger left, his blood filling the screen as the heroine screamed, I lost my heart to that immortal boy.

A mysterious throbbing and a pain like hot needles being stuck into my heart swept through me for the first time ever. The feeling didn't subside even when I tried to sleep, and I couldn't get the image of the boy out of my mind.

By the time color was fully restored to the world, Lapis's body was in pieces, and he was taken to a research lab where an elderly scientist carried out an operation to put him back together again. Even though I knew he was immortal, I was so worried about whether he would actually come back that I couldn't sleep.

By the time the operation was successful and Lapis appeared on the screen again at last, I was no longer able to look straight into those blue eyes.

My body was flushed, and I had a strange ticklish feeling all over as though my skin was being stimulated from underneath. My heart hurt so much I thought I might be ill. It was really odd. All I was doing was watching TV, and I couldn't work out why it was having such a strange effect on my body. My entire body was demanding to meet this boy.

"Mummy, I really want to meet him," I begged.

"You can't because he doesn't exist," she answered offhandedly, and chuckled as she got on with folding the laundry.

It felt like she was making fun of me and trying to discourage me. But the idea that he didn't exist merely dredged up an even hotter lump from deep within my entrails.

I immediately understood. I understood that the boy was exactly who he was, including the fact that I could never meet him. And I also understood that I was in love with everything about him.

The mysterious pain and sensation of blood pumping through my body did not subside. I understood that being infected with this kind of throbbing pain was what we call romantic love.

I realized that I was in love for the first time, with someone who lived inside a story.

I was in a sex education class in the fourth year of elementary school when I discovered that I had been conceived by an abnormal method.

The day before we were due to have our first sex education class, my mother showed me an old, faded brown book, pointing at illustrations of bodies while she explained how she and my father had made me. I felt a bit grossed out, but she told me it was part of my education, so I listened intently.

In the sex education class the next day, though, I was taught something completely different. We were made to watch endless videos about the mechanism of artificial insemination and the mystery of bringing a new life into the world.

At first I thought maybe my mother had been lying to me. Surely the teacher wouldn't tell us anything false?

At the end of the class the teacher said gently that if there was anything we didn't understand, we should go to see her, and so after school I secretly went to ask her about it.

After listening to me, she looked perplexed. "Um, well . . . long ago lots of people used to get pregnant that way. I'm sure your mom just wanted you to learn about the history of scientific progress."

"No, she said that that was how I was born."

"Ah . . . well, um . . ."

"Is my mom weird? Maybe she's making it up?"

"Hmm. I know, we have a home visit coming up, so let me talk to her about it then. I'm sure she's just keen for you to study hard, Amane."

But when my teacher came on the home visit, my mother told her frankly that she'd got pregnant with me through sexual intercourse with my father. The flabbergasted teacher let this slip to her colleagues, and now the teachers' lounge was buzzing with it.

Before long the story had spread to the PTA, and a boy taunted me about it, using vulgar language. "You were born after your mom and dad did it, weren't you? That's incest. Ugh, it's so gross!" he said, pretending to puke.

I couldn't say anything to that. I was trying harder than anyone else to stop myself from puking.

Seeing me go bright red and hang my head, the teacher quickly came over.

"Don't say that!" she scolded the boy. "In the past, everybody used to do it."

But the teacher herself had started everything by saying how disgusting it was, so she wasn't fooling anyone.

I had no idea how long ago "long ago" had been—and I also now realized that our red home was a locked room where we lived surrounded by a past frozen in time.

After that, I went to the library every day to learn everything I could about "proper" sex.

> Humans are the only animal that breeds through scientific means.
>
> Research into artificial insemination progressed rapidly during World War II as a result of the crisis caused by men leaving for the front and the consequent drastic reduction in the number of children. However, the provision of semen by men who had left for the front enabled many women back home to become pregnant and have children by means of artificial insemination.
>
> After the war, research into artificial insemination continued to develop. Insemination by artificial means was safer and, with an overwhelmingly higher success rate than copulation, this technology has spread from developed countries to the entire world, and now breeding through copulation has all but disappeared.
>
> Copulation is no longer needed for breeding, but we can see a relic of it in the romantic feelings people experience even now when reaching maturity. People fall in love with characters from books,

animations, and manga, as well as with other people, and these feelings are similar to those during copulation. If their romantic feelings deepen they become sexually excited, in which case they satisfy this urge through masturbation. Some people satisfy their urge in a similar way to the copulation of old, through the joining of their sexual organs (known as "sex").

Now that pregnancy and childbirth occur by scientific means, they are separate from romantic love. When someone wants to have children, they find a partner, then the woman is artificially inseminated and gives birth to the baby in a hospital. The science is not yet sufficiently advanced for men to conceive, so currently the only option is for the woman to carry the pregnancy. Recently, research into artificial wombs has been progressing, and there are hopes that both men and older women no longer able to conceive with their own womb will also soon be able to carry pregnancies to term.

The more books I read and the more I learned about the proper way to procreate, the more doubts I had. Why had my mother gone to all the trouble of deliberately removing the contraceptive device and copulating in order to get pregnant instead of just being artificially inseminated with my father's sperm? Just thinking about it made me feel nauseous.

I no longer spoke much with my mother. She seemed to sense something was wrong, since she stopped constantly bringing up the subject of primitive copulation with me.

One winter's day in the third semester, she was braiding my hair.

"Why did you do it?" I couldn't help asking her.

"What? Is something wrong, Amane?"

"Mom, why didn't you use the normal method to get pregnant with me?"

She gulped and paused her hands, but after a moment she breathed out and continued with the braiding.

"I had a hunch this was coming," she said in a low voice.

I didn't know whether this was an answer, or whether she was talking to herself.

"Look, Amane, it's raining again, just like the day you were born. Back then it was pouring with rain that smelled of summer," she said lightly, and abruptly let go of my hair. "I can't do the braids properly, the right one is thicker than the left one. You're a big girl now, you can do it yourself."

It's not as if I ever asked her to do it, I thought grumpily, and went to school with my hair done up in a bun.

"You look kind of grown-up today, Amane," a friend complimented me.

My mother had always done my hair in girly styles, like a French braid or regular braids, so it must have seemed like a fresh look.

"Yes. I won't have little-girl hair anymore," I answered, pouting.

I had to leave the walled garden my mother had created. I felt, somehow, that I had already taken a step into a new world.

Now that I knew what proper sex was, I was relieved that I'd fallen in love with Lapis. Just imagine if I'd taken my mother's words to heart and fallen in love with a real-life boy!

By the time I got to fifth grade, just about all my classmates were in love with girls or boys from anime or manga.

It was fashionable to buy a cute travel card case and keep pictures cut out from magazines of your crush inside, and then secretly show it only to your closest, most special friends.

When you and a friend were both in love with the same character, it brought you closer together. I was still in love with Lapis, but the TV series had finished, so I couldn't see him anymore, and none of my friends now kept pictures of him in their travel card cases. I was overjoyed, therefore, when my best friend Yumi showed me a cutout picture of him on the classroom balcony after school. We danced around holding hands, commenting on the beautiful color of his eyes and how he had such a charming and sweet boyish voice.

Sometimes I kept chatting with Yumi until the five-o'clock chime, and got a severe telling-off from my mother when I got home. I was happy that someone else loved Lapis and that I'd found this out because I loved him too.

The limited first edition set of discs in bright-blue packaging in which Lapis lived were carefully lined up on my desk in order from the first episode. I always watched these on the small computer in my bedroom. The whirring of the disc inside my computer sounded like his footsteps approaching me.

When I saw him, the hot lump that had formed within me began creeping around my body, and this feeling continued for some time even after I'd turned off the screen and crawled into bed.

It was a mysterious sensation, as though I'd been infected with a pleasurable pain that lived in me like a parasite. This sweet pain moved around inside my body. My chest, my back, the back of my neck, the area below my belly button . . . even the tips of my toes sometimes hurt.

It felt like I was being bitten inside by Lapis. This delighted me, but it also hurt. As I got older and the sweet pain grew more intense, naturally I had to learn how to eject it from my body.

Just before summer vacation, I was at home watching him on my computer.

The sweet pain had been intensifying within me, and it really felt like I was getting sick. The inside of my skin tingled all over my body, but still I couldn't stop looking at him. Staring at him was all I could do. The movement of his eyebrows, the number of times he blinked, the way the breeze ruffled his hair, the tiniest gesture of his fingertips—I watched all of it, committing it to memory.

It occurred to me that I might be able to reduce the pain a little by wrapping my bedsheets around me.

Wearing earphones on a long cord connected to my computer, I snuggled into bed listening to his voice. Wanting to touch and feel him, I twisted the sheet around my legs.

In my body, an organ I'd never used before was throbbing. As if obeying the voice of that organ, I tensed my legs tangled up in the sheet. My body hurt inside, at the point just below my belly button.

I shook my stiffened legs, and had the sensation that all the blood in my body was fizzing and popping, then all the strength drained out of me.

Sex, something I'd only ever read about in old books, must be what had just happened between me and Lapis, I thought.

I roused my body from the languorous feeling I'd been left with after the pleasure had evaporated, scanned the bookcase, and took out the small booklet I'd been given in my health and physical education class.

I turned the pages until I came to the part where, under the words "The Female Body," there was a drawing of a mysterious organ that looked like an insect's face.

When I'd read the booklet, I hadn't been able to understand that these things—the uterus, ovaries, fallopian tubes, vagina—were all there in my own body. It was the same way I didn't really comprehend that things like the liver and pancreas were actually inside of me. They were all distant organs and would stay that way forever, I thought.

I traced the black lines of the illustration with my finger. The part of my lower body that had felt so hot was the middle bit of this insect face, I now understood. Written there was "uterus."

The person I loved who lived in a story had grabbed hold of my uterus and given it a good shake. The body of someone I couldn't touch physically had, in that moment, become connected with my body.

For the first time, I was aware that the mysterious, complex organ in the illustration actually existed in my lower abdomen. It asserted its existence by shaking up my cells from inside my body, just like my heart when I ran or my bladder when I needed to pee.

The feelings of my heart and bladder were familiar, but the throbbing and pain in my uterus was a physical sensation I'd never felt before. I was genuinely delighted that my body could gain access to Lapis by a means other than just looking.

My uterus was still throbbing a little, and I felt lethargic and a bit feverish. That was proof that Lapis and I had joined our bodies, I thought. This organ of mine was meant for Lapis and me to physically connect our bodies, I thought, gently stroking my belly.

* * *

After this strange experience, I was so tired I fell asleep right away. I totally forgot about my homework and was told off by the teacher the next day.

Yumi asked me, "What happened, Amane? It's unlike you to forget to do your homework," but I couldn't bring myself to explain. How could I tell anyone that I'd been busy having sex with a fictional boy?

"Amane, you've got a stain on your skirt," Yumi whispered in my ear. I rushed to the toilet and found my underpants and thighs covered in blood.

I was shocked. My body was still immature, and I'd thought getting my period would be a long way off in the future.

Maybe my body had grown up all of a sudden after I connected it with Lapis yesterday. When I thought of it like that, the blood staining my thighs suddenly seemed precious.

I went to the school infirmary and was given pads and underwear for periods, and changed into sweatpants. When I got home I told my mother straight away that I had got my period, and we went together to the hospital to get a contraceptive device fitted. It hurt a bit, but I was pleased when the doctor told me with a smile, "So you're an adult now."

My mother kept quiet. She hadn't really wanted me to get the contraceptive device fitted, but it was compulsory, so she reluctantly went along with it.

It didn't hurt for long, and I was proud that my body was at last grown-up.

* * *

Going on to junior high, everyone had their own ways of being in love with boys from their favorite stories. Some girls drew pictures of their crushes so they could touch them, while others dressed up like their boyfriends so they could have contact by becoming them.

And boys also had their own ways of being in love with girls from stories.

Our sexuality developed in a sterile space.

There were about five or six kids in my class who were in love with a real person, but they all hung out together. Most of us had clean love with story characters.

Personally, I had always been in love with Lapis and always would be, I thought. I was too fastidious in my sexuality to fall in love with a real person. I believed I would reach adulthood without ever falling in love with a real person. Then I would be artificially inseminated and have a baby and live with my family while continuing to fall in love with fictional characters. I had no grounds for believing this to be the only future for myself, but I did, never doubting it.

After-school club activities were compulsory at my school. The art club had become the de facto "go-home club," the place for those pupils uninterested in joining clubs, and indeed almost no one stayed behind in the art room to paint. I didn't like painting either, so I'd hardly ever been to the club.

One day I happened to go to the art room to hand in an assignment and found my classmate Mizuuchi painting on his own in the empty room.

The door must have made a sound, but he was so focused on his painting that he didn't notice. I didn't want to disturb him but was too curious, so I went to take a look. To my astonishment, he was painting a picture of Lapis!

I bumped into a desk, and he turned around at the sound and looked shocked to see me there. Hastily he turned the picture over.

"Oh, I'm sorry!"

"Did you see it?" he asked in a small voice.

"I did . . . It's Lapis, isn't it?"

Mizuuchi flushed bright red right to the tips of his ears. He looked down and begged in a hoarse voice, "Yes . . . but don't tell anyone. Please?"

"I won't. And it's a really good picture! I like him too. Look!" I said, showing him the picture I always carried in my travel card case.

Mizuuchi's eyes grew round. "You do?"

"Sure! I've been in love with him ever since preschool. He's my first love."

"Your first love . . ." He looked a bit disconcerted, then said quietly, "Same here."

I was really pleased. It was wonderful that someone else loved the same person I did. I felt like I'd found someone with similar inclinations as me, and was super happy that my boyfriend was loved by someone else too. But Mizuuchi made a sour face and looked down.

"Promise you won't tell anyone that, either. I always say I've never been in love."

"Why? What's wrong with it?"

I didn't understand. I knew some kids hid their love for a real person, but I couldn't fathom why anyone would need to hide their feelings for Lapis.

"Because it's weird. It would be okay if I was in love with a girl, like all the other boys . . . But I love Lapis."

"It's not weird at all. Some of my friends like other girls too, you know."

"I guess . . ."

"Some are in love with real people, others with fictional people. I didn't think anyone really cared about the difference between boys and girls."

"Everyone's always talking about their lovers, aren't they? I just can't. It's private, not something to gossip about with everyone."

I was taken aback and felt a bit ashamed of myself.

"You're so grown-up, Mizuuchi. I'm always telling people about Lapis. I need an outlet for my feelings, I guess. He's the love of my life, and I'm not afraid to let everyone know."

"Maybe I'm more of a child than you. I just can't talk about it."

"It must be because he's so precious to you that you hide your feelings. I mean, there are some things about my love I want to keep secret too. You really do love Lapis, don't you, Mizuuchi?"

Mizuuchi gave a tiny nod.

"You know, I always wonder how everyone can call the person they love just a 'character.' I mean, I just can't do that."

"Me neither. After all, Lapis is Lapis. I don't want to ever make him sound like a kind of toy. I always think about him as someone from the other world."

"The other world?"

"I can't go to the world where Lapis lives, and I can't fight alongside him there. But I have the feeling that his world is always close by."

"Yes, somewhere near but far. Like the dark forest."

"What do you mean?"

"It's an old song. It was on a CD that Mom used to play for me when I was little."

"Ah. But that's my feeling about the place where Lapis lives. He's alive there, and fighting. I always say Lapis and his friends are alive in the 'other world.' And those of us in 'this world' feel it and are crazy about him too, you and me both."

"Oh, I see. I'm going to talk about the 'other world' too. Do you mind if I copy you?"

"It's not like I made it up myself," Mizuuchi said, sounding a little shy.

Mizuuchi and I started talking about Lapis and showing each other our treasures in the art room when nobody else was around. I even swapped my file folders with Lapis printed on them and my cutout pictures of Lapis for Mizuuchi's drawings of him.

"Seriously? You'll swap those for my drawings?" he asked, blushing, but I really did like them.

Mizuuchi drew his pictures with a mechanical pencil, using lots of fine lines and smudging bits of the picture. They always showed Lapis looking right at you.

"He always looks so cool in your pictures, Mizuuchi. How come you're so good at drawing? You're amazing!"

"It's not so much that I'm drawing Lapis, it's that in my head I'm touching him with the tip of my pencil, and when I do that, he appears on the paper. So whenever I want to touch him, I make a drawing."

I felt more envious than ever. With this method, Mizuuchi could touch Lapis whenever he wanted. I tried to emulate him, but it didn't work for me.

"Just one drawing isn't a fair swap. I've got loads more at home. You can have as many as you want."

"Really?"

After school I went over to Mizuuchi's house with him. His closet was stuffed full of sketchbooks.

"I only fell for him after watching the repeats on TV, so I don't have any magazine cutouts or anything like you do, Sakaguchi. So instead I have to draw him myself."

"You love him so much, don't you?" Something else suddenly occurred to me. "Have you ever had sex with him?" I asked. "How do boys do it?"

"What?!" Mizuuchi looked up from rummaging through his sketchbooks and turned to me in surprise. "With Lapis?! Is that even possible?"

"You mean you haven't?"

"'Course not!" He looked embarrassed. "I mean, it said on the news the other day that these days even people who are in love with each other don't do it anymore."

"Yeah, that's true. But I did."

"How?" he asked nervously.

When I explained it to him, he looked embarrassed. "Um, well, isn't that . . . er, masturbation?"

"What? I thought it was sex, the kind I read about in an old book. I was sure I'd had sex with Lapis!"

"I'm not doubting you, but I think what you did is a bit different. I mean, sex is copulation, isn't it? But even adults don't do it anymore. There's no need . . ."

"Oh . . ." I felt deflated. I'd been so happy about having connected with Lapis, but now I was being told I hadn't really done it.

"I want to be a doctor when I grow up. I want to research artificial insemination and artificial wombs so that men can get pregnant too."

"Wow, that's amazing!"

"Then anyone will be able to have a baby on their own. There won't be any need to make a new family. I want to live with Lapis in the future. Ideally, I want to share a home with him and raise a child together."

"You've even thought it that far through . . . You have my full respect, Mizuuchi. You're totally in love with him, aren't you?"

He looked uncomfortable. "But you are too, Sakaguchi."

"Hmm . . . I'm a bit weird, I guess. I thought I'd had sex with him, but apparently I haven't really," I said, feeling miserable.

"But you believe you did, so that means you did," he said.

I felt a strange sensation, a familiar heavy pain in my inner organs. It was only after I'd left Mizuuchi and was on my way home along my regular school route that I realized I'd felt turned on by a real person for the first time. I could vividly recall the way Mizuuchi had peered into my face and the movement of his tongue dampening his dry lips, and again I felt the dull ache in my innards. I stopped in my tracks, dumbfounded. This pain was sexual arousal, I realized. It was exactly the same reaction as I had to Lapis.

When I got home, I took the Tupperware boxes containing the meal my mother had prepared for me out of the refrigerator.

My mother worked late, so I was always alone in the evening. The house felt like it was covered in the sticky fingerprints of her soul, and I was relieved that I couldn't see her face.

I knew I should be grateful to her for having raised me all alone, but I always had an intense urge to throw up when I ate her home-cooked food.

At the sight of her meat-stuffed green peppers, potato salad, and dashi-flavored egg roll in the Tupperware boxes, I felt the nausea welling up again. It mixed unpleasantly with the arousal I'd felt earlier, and my innards started churning.

I gave up on the idea of eating and flushed the food down the toilet. I was hungry, but I didn't feel like putting anything in my mouth.

Maybe this house had put a curse on me, I thought as I watched the egg and peppers being sucked away.

My mother was trying to inculcate me with the instincts she believed in. But I believed that my true instincts were different and already existed somewhere inside me.

Until now I'd thought my purest instinct was the sexual attraction I felt for Lapis. I'd taken solace in the fact that my arousal was something consistent with what society deemed common sense.

But maybe I was wrong. Maybe my mother was right and the instinct of wanting to have sex with the man I loved, and to get pregnant by committing incest with my husband—someone in my own family—was deep within my being. If my weird sexuality went contrary to societal norms, I would probably spend my life being dragged around by it.

I wanted to know my own truth, however harsh it was. I wanted to expose the true instincts in my own body, not the ones my mother had instilled in me or those that society had fostered.

I wanted to find out my true sexual urges. And to do so, I had to have sex with Mizuuchi. Would I want to get pregnant and have his baby? And what did that even mean? I wanted to get everything out in the open. I would go to any lengths to find out.

Coming out of the toilet I felt suffocated, so I undid the buttons on my shirt, loosened the hook on my bra, and lay down on my bed. All I could think about was how I could seduce Mizuuchi into entering my body.

Over six months passed before I had sex with Mizuuchi.

I don't know if what we did could really be called sex, though, as when we were doing it he was expressing his passion for Lapis, not for me.

Since I'd been open with Mizuuchi about my feelings from the start, he seemed to let his guard down and started consulting me about his body. Like me, he experienced a sensation of heat when he thought about Lapis.

My body also always responded to Mizuuchi, but I tried to hide this from him. Yumi and my other friends said loving another person was dirty, but I didn't think so. Rather, with Mizuuchi my desire seemed to get purer and more refined with time.

"If only I could connect my body with Lapis!" Mizuuchi sighed.

I couldn't let this opportunity pass. "Well, shall we try it?"

"What? But Sakaguchi, you only do it on your own so—"

"That's why we should do it together. We should offer our bodies to Lapis. Sex is like a sort of ritual to make an offering of feelings to someone far away, like in the other world. We both love Lapis, and I'm sure he'll be pleased if two people who love him do it together."

I was making everything up as I went along, but Mizuuchi seemed intrigued. "Really? Will our feelings really reach him in the other world?"

"Yes, I read it in a book. Adults are always doing it, that's what the book said. Come on, let's try!"

I tried every argument I could think of, but it took a month for Mizuuchi to be convinced.

At the end of autumn, the day before the start of winter break in our first year in junior high, we were sitting in the deserted art room after the school-closing ceremony, talking about Lapis.

"Talking about Lapis like this, I can feel my heart beat faster. What about you, Mizuuchi?"

"Yeah, me too."

"Can you feel your pulse?"

"Do you want to measure it?"

I pressed the vein sticking up in his wrist. "It's really fast!"

"Yeah, it always gets fast when I think about Lapis."

"I always get overwhelmed when I think about Lapis too. Hey, why don't we try the ritual to offer him our feelings? I think I could do it with you, Mizuuchi, if it means I can really offer my love to Lapis."

"I dunno . . ." He tilted his head and looked doubtful, but he didn't seem to be rejecting the idea.

"Come on," I pushed him, "let's make an offering of our feelings to Lapis. We have to think about Lapis and make our bodies like grown-ups. If we do that, it'll work. I read all about it in a book."

"What do you mean, grown-ups?"

"Like, maybe our pulses will beat faster?"

"Won't we die?"

"I don't know."

I suggested we go straight home, and Mizuuchi obediently followed. I felt like I was abducting him.

Since it was a weekday, my mother wasn't home. We dropped by the library on the way to borrow a sex education book. Having studied it carefully, we decided to do what it said.

It didn't say anything about foreplay, so we started straight away by attempting penetration.

The male body was simple, with a sex organ that was easy to understand. Mizuuchi had apparently already experienced his first ejaculation, and he quickly produced an erection, as if by magic.

I knew that we had to insert that into me, but my sex organ was harder to understand. The illustration in the book was simple and clear, but when I looked at the actual thing in a mirror, it was like some strange creature I'd never seen before was stuck between my legs. I couldn't make head or tail of it, no matter how much I compared it to the illustration in the book.

"Anyway, I guess we should start by looking for this vaginal opening."

"Yeah, but which one is it? I can't see it at all."

We started searching for the vaginal opening together.

"I dunno," Mizuuchi said.

I looked in the mirror too, but I couldn't tell where the opening was either. "Is this it?"

"Isn't that for peeing?"

"What about this one? I can get my finger in there, anyway."

"Will it really fit in there?"

I'd had no idea that such an inexplicable place existed in my body. I wasn't at all sure I was right, but there wasn't anywhere else, so we tried sticking it in there, though at first I couldn't find the mysterious cavity where I'd put my finger before. By trial and error, after numerous attempts, Mizuuchi finally managed to get his part into my body.

"We finally did it!"

"I guess this is right?"

We decided to leave things at that for today.

The next time we tried, Mizuuchi ejaculated. As his body stiffened and he held his breath, I felt something warm flow into my body.

"Seems like my body has finished the ritual," Mizuuchi said, pulling his organ out of my body.

"There's still something coming out of it."

A clear liquid, like water, was still trickling out of Mizuuchi, as though he hadn't managed to get it all out.

We had both been fitted with contraceptive devices, and what was coming out of Mizuuchi looked like water.

In the book it had said, "When the sexual organ has not been fitted with a contraceptive device, a cloudy white liquid is discharged through the external urethral opening." But it hadn't said anything about a clear liquid, so we found this very confusing.

I touched the liquid with my finger, which I then licked. The taste was faintly medicinal.

"I wonder why this liquid is coming out?"

We'd both read books about it, but neither of us could get our heads around how people in the old days used to get impregnated.

"I don't know why, but it feels good when it does, doesn't it? So maybe that's why?"

"But then the bed gets dirty, so it'd be much better if it didn't come out," he said, annoyed.

I was fascinated by this strange liquid. Nothing like it had ever come out of me, so I quizzed Mizuuchi about it.

"What does it feel like? Does it feel hot? Different from when you go to the bathroom?"

"Yeah. When it comes out, for a moment it feels really good, and then my body feels really quiet."

"Wow, how strange."

"What about you, Sakaguchi? How do you make your body go quiet?"

"Um, I don't really know."

My body probably hadn't yet developed enough to get hot like Mizuuchi's did, and the sensation of something exploding inside me when I'd had sex with Lapis hadn't happened with Mizuuchi, so I still didn't really understand what he meant.

"And how does your body get noisy?" I asked him.

"I'm not sure it does . . . I can't really explain it very well, but it's kind of like all the little hairs all over me are being pulled upward so my whole body feels excited. It's a really weird feeling," he explained in a serious voice.

After that, we had sex, or what we called sex, many times, but other than pain and slight relief, I still didn't feel anything.

Part of me was reassured. My main objective in wanting to have sex with Mizuuchi had been to discover the nature of my own sexual urges.

I was frightened by the thought that I might one day be seized with the urge to copulate with a real person and have a baby, like my mother had drummed into me time and time again since I was little. The possibility that falling in love with Mizuuchi was a sign of this future was terrifying.

But in the end, what we did was a far cry from copulating to get pregnant, like in my mother's old books. The sensation was more in the brain, and I was relieved. My fears were allayed by the fact that my instinct took the form accepted by society.

The feeling that we were exploring inside each other's bodies was fun, and I invited Mizuuchi over very often after that. And I could confirm the form of my own sexual urges any number of times.

* * *

My mother had copulated with my father to become pregnant with me. As I grew into adulthood I came to understand what this actually meant, and I found it even more creepy.

I was naturally more enthusiastic about "ordinary" love.

Mizuuchi went on to a private senior high school, while I went to a normal school. Our email exchanges grew more and more sporadic and eventually stopped altogether, but by then I'd fallen in love again. My new lover used an arm bracelet to transform himself into a champion of justice to keep world peace.

I loved boys from the other world as well as real-life boys. These two types of love had lots of things in common and lots of differences.

Sexual love with a real person had taste and smell. I could swallow their sperm and breathe in their sweat. But falling in love with a real person felt like I was numb from an anesthetic, and I never felt the sort of vividness that Yumi was always talking about, which was kind of mysterious too.

Sexual love with someone in a story was solely a conversation with my own flesh. The pain I felt in my body and my hunger to meet them troubled me, but this pain and hunger were also very dear to me.

With either type of person, even just the thought of my lover made my womb hurt. Either way, I engaged in sex as though being dragged around by that pain.

Time and time again I had to confirm that the sexual desire I felt was different from the "fall in love and have babies" that my mother had inculcated in me as a child.

Penetration with my real-life lover was always quiet, a far cry from copulation. This was me having sex using parts of the body that I understood were entirely unrelated to procreation. It was a relief when I confirmed this.

Among my real-world lovers, many had never had sex. Probably most of them, in fact. They were all surprised when I showed them the vaginal opening that I'd had to search for with Mizuuchi.

The art teacher who became my lover almost as soon as I started high school was the same.

"Why have you never had sex, Sensei?"

"Um, I suppose because there was never any need. You're unusual, Sakaguchi. From what I hear, young people now do it even less than my generation."

"I see."

"You must have learned about it in class, right? Copulation was the norm before the war, but when adult men were sent off to fight, research into artificial insemination progressed rapidly in order to produce lots of children for the war effort. People stopped going to all the bother of copulating like animals. We're a more advanced creature now."

"I know all that, but . . . when you fall in love, don't you ever feel the urge to have sex?"

"Well, I guess some people do, but generally sex is a relic of old-fashioned copulation. Even when people do fall in love, most of them deal with their libido by themselves."

True, hardly anyone my age did anything resembling copulation. I'd heard older people talking about it, but pretty much everyone in my generation now handled sexual gratification alone.

"Sensei, have you ever imagined a world that is parallel to this one? Everyone would still be copulating if there hadn't been so much progress in artificial insemination, wouldn't they?"

"Hmm, probably only reluctantly, though. After all, if that was the only way to procreate, then people would have no choice but to resort to primitive copulation. But still, there's no point imagining that. The human race has advanced."

Sensei smiled and stroked my hair as if to say I talked about the strangest things.

Sex was disappearing. My mother's world was already vanishing. Serves her right, I thought.

The world was changing fast. I found that change refreshing.

At my new school I quickly made friends with Juri, who was in the same class and after-school club as me. She was beautiful. She looked half-foreign, with her finely chiseled features and eyes that were impressively large even without mascara.

Her eyelashes and pupils were a bright, deep black and always looked as though they were moist like after rain.

She stood out so much that even boys from other schools would lie in wait for her to confess their love, but she curtly rejected them all. She was laid-back and easy to talk to. We hit it off, and both joined the school's art club, so we spent every day together. Like in my old school, the art club was quite easygoing unless we had an exhibition coming up. Many of the more senior pupils never bothered turning up, but Juri was serious about painting, so I would stay too, and the two of us often had the art room to ourselves for long periods.

One day I was reading a book about ceramics that I'd found lying around, snacking on some sweets that a senior had left for us, while Juri painted one of the watercolors she was so good at. She heated up some water in a kettle hidden in the room, poured some over a teabag, and passed me a mug.

"Thanks." The tea smelled of jasmine.

"Amane," she suddenly said, lowering her voice. "Have you ever had a boyfriend?"

I looked at her in surprise. She'd always looked bored whenever the conversation turned to love, and sometimes excused herself on the grounds of having something else to do, so I'd never have thought she would start that sort of conversation.

"Sure." I'd already split up with my teacher by then and had another lover.

She looked surprised. "I don't mean just a regular boyfriend. I mean a proper lover."

"Yep, both my first and second boyfriends were lovers—we had sex."

"What? You've had sex?"

"Sure."

"How old were you?"

"I was in the fifth year of elementary school."

Juri looked taken aback for a moment. "You mean real sex?" she asked, looking a little puzzled. "What was he like?"

"I'm pretty sure you must have seen him before, Juri. He was really popular back then. His name was Lapis. He had silver hair and blue eyes, and was a boy who was seven thousand years old."

Juri looked relieved. "Oh, you mean that anime character."

"Well, yeah, but we had a physical relationship too. One day I was longing for him so much I put my key chain with his picture on it in my mouth!"

"That doesn't count as sexual intercourse! Even if you went further than that, it's only masturbation."

"You really think so?"

"When it boils down to it, anime characters like him are only tools to turn us on and simulate romance. All you did was use him as a tool to simulate love and to help you masturbate."

I was a bit offended at my first love being called a tool, and shut my mouth, sulking.

"I'm sorry, Amane," she said in a soothing voice. "I know this was important for you. But you shouldn't really say things like this. From other people's point of view, it's just masturbation, not sex."

"If you say so."

Mizuuchi had said the same thing.

"So the second time was with an anime character too, I suppose?"

"No, that was a real person. A guy in my class in the first year of junior high. I had sex with him too."

Taken aback, Juri pressed on, asking whether I had actually put his penis in me. When I told her exactly what had happened, she frowned in distaste.

"That really was sex, then," she said. "I don't know how you could do something as dirty as that."

"Dirty? I loved him and thought his tongue and penis were the prettiest things in the whole world."

She looked stunned. "So you must be the kind of person that falls in love, Amane. You seem so young for your age, I never expected that," she said, and poured some more tea into her empty mug.

"The kind of person that falls in love? Maybe I am."

Now that she mentioned it, I was always falling in love. I'd been in love ever since kindergarten, either with real-life people or ones from other worlds, and been dragged around by my own flesh. Romantic love and my body were always linked.

"That is utterly inconceivable for me," said Juri. "I don't want to fall in love with anyone in my entire life. I want to have a child, so I'll probably get married, but I know I will never ever have sex."

"Hmm, okay."

Not many of the girls in high school fell in love with real people, and even most of those who did had never had sex. Most of the girls in our class were virgins. Our classmates Mika and Emiko were crazy about anime characters and had never gone out with a real boy.

"These days, you don't have to fall in love with someone in order to breed," Juri went on calmly, "so all sorts of anime characters have been created for our sexual gratification. They're just consumables to help us process our desire. And everyone's fine with that. It won't be long before nobody bothers to have sex anymore. It's very unhygienic, after all."

"Seriously?"

"Sex and love will soon disappear altogether. Now that babies are all made by artificial insemination, there's no need to go to all that trouble."

I'd seen on the news the other day that fewer people were having sex. Apparently, 80 percent of our generation would reach adulthood without ever having had sex. Even if people fell in love and formed couples, that didn't necessarily mean they were coupling their sexual organs. There wasn't any need.

But when I fell in love with a real person, without fail I had them put their penis into my vagina. I'd just done it with my new lover after splitting up with my teacher—my third lover, or my twenty-eighth if you counted all the nonreal people. It wasn't that I was fixated on genitalia; it's just that I somehow always ended up wanting to do it. Even though sex was less popular, it wouldn't ever vanish altogether, I thought to myself, although I never actually said so to others.

"You've also made use of quite a few anime characters yourself, haven't you, Amane? In order to masturbate," she said, rather judgmentally. "Anyway, I don't have a problem with that. It's a lot cleaner than having sex."

"That's not how I think of it. Once I fall in love, I never dispose of that lover. I love them for the rest of my life. My feelings crystallize in my body, so when I fall in love with someone, they will be my lover forever."

"Oh, don't be so childish, Amane. Those anime characters are like idols, created expressly to excite us sexually and to help pleasure us down there. Don't call them lovers, it creeps me out."

I went over to my bag, took out a drawstring purse, and went back over to Juri.

"What are you doing?"

Without answering, I opened the purse and took out key chains and laminated cutout pictures one by one and laid them out on the desk in front of her.

"This is Lapis. He was the first to teach me how to love. This is Kilt. He has an exceptionally strong sense of justice and taught me the importance of staying true to myself. This is

Roku Ryusui. Terrible things have happened to him his whole life, but he doesn't hold any grudges and is kind to everyone, and he taught me about how wonderful it is to empathize with people. This is Bruma. He is very mysterious, but all the same he risks his life fighting alone for the main character. He taught me the preciousness of friendship. This . . ."

Juri sat there dumbfounded as I laid out all twenty-five lovers from the other world.

I looked her straight in the face. "Loving them, I have learned super important things as a human being. They are all a precious part of me. None of them are at all disposable! All my lovers are important to me, in fact they're my heroes. Falling in love with them made me who I am. I wouldn't be who I am without them. And what's more—" I started choking up but kept it together. "What's more, they have saved me when times have been tough, when I've been sad. We live all together. And we'll live together forever. They're super important to me as lovers, as friends. So don't say nasty things about them."

None of my friends would ever say anything like this. Even girls who fell in love with people from the other world like I did still called them "characters" and felt superior to them.

But I wanted to stay true to myself. Lapis would never have been discouraged by this sort of thing, I told myself. Having bared a precious part of my heart, I stood there feeling embarrassed.

Juri said nothing for a while, then said quietly, "Well, you'd better put those twenty-five important lovers back in your purse.

"What?"

I looked up uncomprehendingly and saw her staring at my lovers, her long eyelashes fluttering.

"If you show something that's dear to you to other people, that thing can quite easily get trampled out of shape. If they are so important to you, you should keep them shut away."

Juri still looked down on classmates who were infatuated, but she never said anything bad about me again after that.

"I don't know why," she said, "but you were absolutely terrifying that time, Amane. There's something about you that I don't understand at all. And I don't want to."

I was glad that Juri could talk about things objectively and at least try to understand. I felt I could tell her about my love life without holding anything back, and she in turn could confide in me about her plans for the future. We became close friends, sharing our deepest secrets with each other, and we stayed friends even after graduating from high school.

As I grew into adulthood I continued to fall in love with both real and nonreal people.

When I was old enough, I wanted to leave home as soon as possible, but it was hard to make a living without a proper job, and my mother didn't seem in any hurry for me to leave.

I finally managed to leave home after I finished college and found a job.

I was hired by a company that supplied construction materials, like onsite scaffolding, working in their office in an old building in Nihonbashi, central Tokyo. Once I'd got used to the work, I started wanting to have a baby, and so at age twenty-five I married a man I met at a matchmaking party.

However, our relationship didn't last long, and we soon got divorced.

We had taken both our jobs into consideration and planned for me to be artificially inseminated on my twenty-eighth birthday. He was properly set up with a long-term lover, and our respective lovers both came to congratulate us at our wedding ceremony.

He had always liked to stroke my head. We both liked movies, so we often watched them together. He was in the habit of stroking my head while watching them, as though petting a dog, nothing untoward about it. But then one day this action suddenly became sexual. I noticed his hand beginning to move differently than usual and thought it must just be my imagination, but then he abruptly started fondling my bottom and breasts. As I struggled to my feet, his erect penis touched my knee.

I was horrified. I'd never imagined that a member of my own family would have an erection because of me. I tried to scream, but he covered my mouth with his. I felt my tongue being licked all over, and nausea welled up within me. I vomited into his mouth, and as he recoiled I pushed him away and ran into the toilet, where I threw up again and again.

I went straight to the police. They were shocked when I told them that I'd been sexually assaulted by my husband, and sheltered me. They said I had better not go back home until things had settled down, so I took refuge at Juri's for a while, since I thought my mother would probably take my husband's side. Juri told me I should press charges against him, but I didn't even want to see his face again, so I didn't go that far. I looked for a cheap studio apartment and took some time off work during the week to collect my belongings from the home we had shared. That was how I started living alone.

When we divorced, our respective families got together to discuss what had happened.

His parents gave him a good grilling as he sat hanging his head. "That's the sort of thing people only do outside the home. I can't believe you tried to have sex with your wife!"

My mother, meanwhile, was strangely calm. "Well, these things can happen."

After the divorce had gone through, I didn't really feel like falling in love again. My lovers from the other world, who had been with me since childhood, were the ones who consoled me for having been soiled.

Their existence purified me. I felt so grossed out that I couldn't imagine being with a real person ever again.

I thought I'd stay living with them like that in my germ-free room, but my vague longing to have a child didn't go away.

I didn't think it was possible financially to raise a child alone. When I told Juri that I was going to give up on the idea, she told me sharply, "You have to do the things in life that you want. Don't worry, perverts wanting to commit incest with their wife are very rare. Just look around and see who you find. You don't have to make up your mind right away, do you?"

Feeling persuaded, I went to another matchmaking party. I was thirty-one years old.

"You already failed once. Why bother again?" my other friends said, but Juri's sharp words had given me confidence.

I went to the party with a friend who was also looking for a partner, and that's where I met my current husband.

The party had been advertised as "Most popular! Limited to people in their thirties, standard marriage party ☆" with the following conditions: "Must be thirty-something, want a child, and want both partners to work. Must agree to equal share of housework and household budget, be willing to purchase an apartment in Tokyo, and have a minimum annual income of four million yen. Lovers and sex in the home STRICTLY FORBIDDEN."

As the safest, best-known matchmaking party available, it was popular with newcomers, and very crowded.

Before going, you had to input details such as: Do you prefer a partner who likes cooking or cleaning? Which TV programs do you like watching in the morning? Do you want the TV to be on at mealtimes? What time do you go to sleep?

Do you want to have separate bedrooms? Participants who were a greater than 95 percent match were marked with a star ☆ next to their name. My second husband was one of three men with a star.

Of the three, I felt that my husband, who was a year younger than me, was the cleanest and most likely to be comfortable to live with. To the question of whether he wanted to spend more on clothes, food, or the home, he had chosen food and wasn't so interested in the others, and he had stated that he preferred to stay at home rather than travel for the New Year and summer vacations, which also matched my tastes.

My friend sat next to me at the party. She had twelve starred people, maybe because she'd chosen the most popular conditions, such as taking a vacation abroad every year, turning off the light when going to sleep, and no need for either partner to do any cleaning beyond switching on the Roomba, and as a result she was struggling to narrow her choices down. In that sense you could say that my husband and I were lucky.

"Hello, I'm Saku Amamiya."

"Nice to meet you. I'm Amane Sakaguchi. Saku, the new moon—that's a nice name."

"I was born on the day of the new moon, so it's the simplest possible name my parents could have given me."

"Snap—it was raining when I was born, which is how I got to be called Amane, the sound of the rain. So we've both got simple names."

We had three minutes to talk together before moving onto the next candidate, so we didn't get the chance to say much more than that, but he didn't leave a bad impression. I couldn't really remember anything about the other two starred people, so I wrote his number down as my first choice, and we were set up as a couple and our contacts were exchanged.

We met up for dinner when we had days off, and on our third date we decided to get married.

The deciding factor was my telling him about my first marriage. When I explained the circumstances behind my divorce, Saku frowned.

"That's just terrible! Making sexual advances on your own family member, of all things!" He thought a moment, then said hesitantly, "If it's not too traumatic or difficult, would you mind telling me what happened? I think it's important that as family members we share the burden of the wound."

As we sat there in the cafe drinking tea together, I told him everything without holding anything back.

He listened, and then felt sick and had to rush to the toilet to throw up. We went into the unisex toilet where there was enough room for a wheelchair, and I rubbed his back while he vomited.

"I'm sorry. You're the one who was hurt, not me . . ." He apologized repeatedly, oozing sweat. "Just hearing about it makes me ill . . . The very idea of a married couple having sex, it's horrifying!"

Seeing him apologizing for being in such a state when I was the victim, not him, made me feel that I would be okay with this man.

And so, my husband and I became family.

As soon as we were married, we moved into a rented apartment in Higashi Nihonbashi. My husband's workplace was a little far away, with several train transfers, but the apartment was close to the station and sunny.

We decided that I would be artificially inseminated once I turned thirty-five, and we also started saving to buy a house.

Everything went smoothly. When I reported this to my mother, she said only half-jokingly, "A marriage that goes too smoothly gives me the creeps."

PART TWO

I was walking along the wet asphalt at night, the gray streets turning black in the rain. The puddles looked like India ink in the dark, while parts touched by light from the streetlamps were a pale gray. It was like walking through an ink painting.

When I got home, the lights were on, and I thought that my husband must already be back. Opening the door, I was met with air that carried a faint trace of someone else's body heat. It smelled different from the dusty chill that had greeted me when I was living alone. I liked that sensation. I was so glad I'd married him.

As I went into the room lightly infused with my husband's body heat, I saw that he was asleep on the sofa.

I stroked his head. His hair was soft and pleasing to the touch. We'd once looked after a neighbor's pale-blue budgie when I was little, and my husband somehow reminded me of that little bird. He was smooth to the touch, smart, and hardly smelled of anything. Even his excrement barely seemed human, and I was not repelled by it in any way.

I noticed a small love bite on his neck. He must have just come from his lover. I stared at the mark, amused.

"Saku," I said, gently shaking his shoulder. "If you sleep here, you'll catch a cold."

He opened his eyes a crack. "Amane, you're home." He had dry, powdery sleep stuck to his eyelashes.

"Close your eyes," I said, and brushed the sleep off. "Weren't you going on a date tonight? You're home early."

Crumpled on the table was a woman's handkerchief. My husband always brought something of his lover's home with him after a date. He said having it helped a little with his state of mind during the time he couldn't see her.

My husband fell in love as easily as I did, although he only loved real people. His current girlfriend was the sixth since we had married three years ago, but he hadn't yet got used to being in love and it was painful.

I too was having a painful love affair at the moment. I carried men around in my bag. I didn't have a real-life lover these days, but I still had all my other ones. Nothing had changed from the time I kept my lovers in a drawstring purse. Now I carried fragments of them around in a black Prada pouch.

Yesterday, when I counted them, there were exactly forty. Thinking how I'd lived so much of my life in love, I felt almost unbearable affection for both my life and for them.

When I married my husband, both he and I had real-life lovers, and we invited them to our wedding. My husband's girlfriend at the time was quiet and pretty, with long hair. Even now, we kept the photo of the four of us in our wedding album.

My husband had aged quite a lot since then. Maybe he was just haggard from love. I crouched down beside the sofa and peered into his pale face.

"Did you have a fight with her or something?"

"No, no, it's nothing like that, but . . . she's already started to lose interest in me. But she can't bring herself to tell me. Instead, she cuts her wrists."

"Did she cut them today too? Was she okay? Did she go to the hospital?" I asked, concerned.

I'd met my husband's current girlfriend a few times too. She was petite, with short hair, and I was entertained by the way she chatted so breezily and cheerfully with my husband. The three of us laughed a lot while having dinner together.

There was a rather sharp side to her too, but she was a smart, lovely woman, and I liked her. She and my husband seemed happy together, and I warmly encouraged their love.

Lately, though, whenever I suggested the three of us go out to dinner together, it somehow never worked out. I couldn't imagine that lively woman being such a wreck now. Even just hearing about it was hard.

"Don't worry, she's only doing it to show me her blood. If she doesn't do that, the love she has for me will steadily extinguish until she forgets all about me." His face was as white as the handkerchief he was clutching in his hand.

"Shall I make some hot tea? It'll help to calm you down."

"Thank you," he said, his voice hoarse, "You are the only family I have in this world. You are the one person I can never fall in love with."

"Of course! We're a married couple. Hold on a moment, I'll go get the tea. I'll be right back."

I made some hot green tea in a mug and took it to him.

"I feel a little better now, thank you." He sipped his tea then closed his eyes tightly and quietly said, "It's only when I'm at home that I don't need to be in love."

I nodded. "That's right. Me too, when I'm here with you like this, Saku, I can truly forget there's such a thing as love in the world," I said, gently stroking his hair.

He looked comfortable, sitting with his eyes closed. "I want to have a baby soon. I have the feeling that if I had a child, I could be free of this madness."

"You want to bring our plan forward? I think we'd still be in time if we make an appointment for artificial insemination now."

"No, it'll be hard for you to take maternity leave until you change departments, won't it, Amane? And we have to save up money, as we've discussed."

"Well, yes, there is that."

"Love is love, and family is family, right? Let's keep to our plan for artificial insemination next year. I'm sorry for complaining." He gave a little smile. "I'm looking forward to having a child. Once we have a child, maybe I'll stop falling in love and get healthy."

"That would be great."

"Did you go on a date today, Amane?"

I nodded. "Yep, I did. I don't have a real-life lover at the moment, but that means I have dates every night."

"Are you happy?"

"Yes, I am," I said without hesitation. Dating wasn't always easy, but it did bring me joy.

"I'm so glad. I'm happy your love life is going well, Amane."

My husband raised the pale, dry skin on his cheeks into a smile, and closed his eyes wearily.

The condo Juri had been living in since she got married was about a five-minute walk from Hanzomon Station in central Tokyo.

We had attended different universities, but we'd kept in touch and still met up even after we'd both got married. Juri's husband often worked weekends, which made meeting up easier, and I had the impression we got together even more often than in college.

As I climbed the slope past a small shrine, her large white building came into view. To my eyes it looked like a luxurious and happy place to live, but Juri said that it wasn't so great, as there weren't any shops nearby and it was a bit creepy on weekends, when there was hardly anyone around.

Her three-bedroom apartment was stuffed full of antique furniture that Juri and her husband had been given when her husband's cousin got divorced. Juri grumbled that she'd at least wanted to choose her own furniture, but seeing her sitting among all these high-quality items, I couldn't help thinking she looked like a princess in a dollhouse like the one I used to play with as a child.

Juri's baby was sleeping peacefully in her crib, wrapped in an organic cotton blanket. Juri was still nursing, so she had decaf tea while I had black tea to accompany the peach tart she'd made.

Glancing sideways at her baby, she said with a sigh, "To tell the truth, I wish I could have married you, Amane."

"What?" I blinked in surprise.

She shrugged. "After all, when it comes to a sperm donor, you can just use a sperm bank these days, can't you? The basis for choosing a partner is all about the balance of each partner's contribution to income and housework, whether you can trust them, whether you can talk to them . . . It all boils down to your gut feelings on these points, doesn't it? It's far more common to find a suitable partner by selecting your various requirements on matchmaking sites or at parties than it is to marry a male friend. But we're talking about choosing a life partner! Is a hunch enough for that? Wouldn't it make far more sense to start a family with a friend you've known since high school?"

"I guess it would. If same-sex marriage was allowed, I'd have liked to marry you too, Juri. I've known you for ages and feel secure with you, and we would be able to share childcare and housework well. And what about Yuki and Naomi? They even went abroad so they could get married, didn't they?"

"That's right! But it's a bit crazy that they had to go that far."

"Why does our country keep insisting on only recognizing marriages between men and women? It's so behind the times!"

"Well obviously, it's because only women have wombs." Juri's moist eyes narrowed as she smiled, squashing the black holes of her pupils below her pure-white eyelids. "If it were possible for male same-sex couples to have children, I bet the number of man-woman marriages would drop fast. Most men would probably be far more comfortable marrying another man, truth be told."

"I wonder. You're probably right."

Come to think of it, she did have a point. Our world was constantly changing. Already, things had changed a lot since Juri and I had first chatted together in high school. Even fewer people were having sex now, and I'd heard that even falling in love with real people was becoming less common in the younger generation.

"That's the way the world is headed, for sure. That's my hunch, anyway. If we'd both been born a hundred years later, I'd definitely have married you, Amane."

Suddenly there was the sound of rain outside.

"That's a heavy shower. It smells of summer," Juri murmured.

I gazed at the street outside the window, now suddenly wet with rain.

That's the sound of the day you were born, Amane, my husband always said whenever he heard rain, and somehow I'd even started hearing the sound of my first cry as a newborn baby superimposed on the sound of rain, although I couldn't possibly have heard such a thing myself.

Did my husband also have the auditory hallucination of my newborn cry whenever he heard the rain? It occurred to me that sharing the five senses like this even when we were apart was what being family meant.

The Chiba Prefecture news was on the TV.

"Chiba has changed a lot, hasn't it? I can hardly believe it's where we first met."

"Well, there's nothing we can do about that," Juri said bluntly. "After all, there's no more Chiba now, just Experiment City. Neither of us lives there now, nor do our parents, so I guess we don't have a hometown anymore."

"True, but that is a rather odd feeling," I said, feeling quite sentimental.

Juri didn't seem to care so much. "Losing our ancestral home is a good thing, you know. We should just live our lives looking forward to the future."

Just then, her daughter, who'd been sleeping swaddled in the cotton blanket, started crying.

"Oh, oh, maybe she's hungry." Juri picked her up and cuddled her. She immediately stopped crying and started giggling. "She's so capricious. Laughing all of a sudden!"

Smiling as she looked into her daughter's face, Juri was the very picture of motherhood.

Outside, the rain had already stopped, and the wet world was gradations of gray.

After enjoying lunch and peach tart at Juri's place, I stayed just long enough to greet her husband when he came home from Sunday overtime at the office. I didn't want to intrude on their family time, but it was also true that I didn't like her husband much.

Juri's husband thought the same way she did. He had never had sex with anyone and said it was a meaningless activity that would eventually disappear. When I heard him and Juri talking about this, I kind of felt that I was being reproached for always falling in love and having sex.

It was still only 3:00 p.m. when I arrived at the station closest to home. The weather was fine and my husband was out on a date. Rather than go home to an empty apartment, I decided to go on a date too, and set off walking in the opposite direction from home.

There was a small river a short walk away, and strolling along the riverside path was really pleasant in such nice weather.

I took my Prada pouch out of my bag and removed the plastic key chain attached to the zipper. The orange-haired boy smiling back at me was my current lover, Krom. I stroked the key chain and gently clasped it in my hand.

Krom was a policeman from the future, and he traveled by time machine to keep world order in different eras. I always eagerly awaited late night on Tuesdays, which was when I could see him.

I often used to be laughed at by friends in high school for going on dates like this with people from the other world. Everyone enjoyed love with anime characters as a form of amusement, but for me it was always painful in a way. When I looked into Krom's eyes, I wanted to join our bodies. I could never fully suppress the passion I felt, and it gnawed away at me.

I sometimes wondered whether the red house I grew up in had put a curse on me to always fall in love so deeply. Even now, I sometimes shuddered at how wet concrete took on a reddish-black hue in the rain.

I squeezed Krom, trying to calm myself down.

The cool plastic slowly warmed up in my hand. Of all my forty lovers, I would take the one that I currently felt most strongly for out of the pouch and affix it to the zipper. That way I could see his face whenever I felt like it and could hold hands with him like this.

I had on occasion walked hand in hand along this path with the four real-life lovers I'd had since getting married. There was a certain charm about a flesh-and-blood hand, but there was also a unique euphoria in holding hands like this with nonreal people.

Romantic love with real people would quickly slip into a feeling of following a manual if you weren't careful: it'd soon be time to start holding hands, and once you've kissed, then this is the next step, et cetera. I knew these things should be decided by both our bodies, but I still couldn't help following the manual seared into my mind.

Love with nonreal people always started with figuring something out: how to start holding hands, how to kiss. I had to work out how to use my own body to access the object of my love. My nails and hair and earlobes—everything was a means to feel my lover on my flesh.

Even walking slowly along the river holding hands with Krom like this was a method I'd come up with by trial and error.

Krom was the one I loved most at the moment, but I still loved all of the lovers I kept in the pouch. Unlike with real people, love with someone who inhabited a story never came to an end or disappeared. Even if it subsided, it stayed frozen in my body and could flare up again at any trigger.

Looking at my pouch with so many lovers in it, I felt my life was extremely rich. I sometimes even thought this small pouch was the world that my soul inhabited.

My low-heeled shoes sank into the soft grass. The smell of earth blended with the smell of water, and their fragrance seeped into the memory of my date with Krom.

A man was sitting on the riverbank while a woman walked her dog and an elderly person took photos of the landscape. They all seemed to be alone, but perhaps they were also secretly on dates with nonreal people.

As if responding to the smile that escaped my lips, the metal fitting on Krom's key chain tinkled. Instantly I felt heat in my inner organs. The cells on the inside of my skin longed to feel the presence of Krom. I hurried home, checked that my husband wasn't there, and in my room greedily had passionate sex with Krom.

Whatever Mizuuchi or Juri said, I called this sex. When I closed my eyes, only Krom was there under my skin. He alone held sway over my inner organs.

The veins running through me were live wires, binding my entire body in tingling heat. I felt Krom's presence connect with my body. This was the sole reason I longed for sex again and again.

My mother despised anyone who loved nonreal people. "You're only shutting yourself up in a pleasant world that is comfortable and clean," she would say. "My way is much better than that."

I had no idea what she meant by "comfortable and clean." I was awash with desire, in pain, and unsightly, but all the same I couldn't stop myself from connecting my body with Krom, however gross that was.

As if spewing heat, I came. Something similar to the clear liquid that Mizuuchi had discharged now turned into gas and belched out of my vagina. I couldn't see it, but my body could feel the vapor coming out of my flesh.

After it was over, Krom returned to the other world, and I couldn't touch him anymore.

However many times I vaporized my feelings of longing for Krom like this, they were never completely exhausted from my body.

Even after I belched out the heat, the sensation of hot water flowing through my veins didn't subside. Gripping the key chain with Krom inside, I softly closed my eyes.

One weekend when my husband was out on a date, I went to visit my mother in Yokohama.

Many people had remained in Chiba when it was made into Experiment City, but my mother was one of those who had left, and she had moved to Yokohama right at the start of the experiment ten years ago. Her condo was small, with only one bedroom, but it was in a new building and was much smarter than the apartment where my husband and I lived.

In there she had the same red furniture as before. I sat down on the sofa feeling sick and tired of her bad taste.

"How have you been?" I asked her.

"My back still hurts, and I can't stand for long in the kitchen."

She was getting old and moved more slowly than before. She had always moved briskly around her home, but now her movements had grown sluggish, as though she was trying to preserve her strength, preparing for hibernation like a bear. That might explain why she'd put on so much weight. Seeing her body encased in fat, I even wondered whether all that talk of having fallen in love and given birth to me when she was young was just a story she'd made up.

I didn't particularly want to see her, but she was lonely and would call saying that her back hurt or she had a headache, urging me to show my face one weekend or on my way home from work. She always told me to bring my husband, but I declined and started dropping by solo once every two or three months.

"Getting old is no fun. I wish you would hurry up and give me a grandchild. I probably won't be around for much longer. And why isn't Saku with you today? I really wanted to see him."

"Saku's on a date today. He hasn't got time to come all the way to Yokohama to listen to you grumbling."

She grimaced at the word "date." "Oh, how filthy of him," she spat. "But never mind, he'll quickly change once you have a child. And don't you go saying it's a matter of timing at work—just go for it. By the time I was your age, you were already going to elementary school and I was working to support us both."

"I know. But Saku and I have decided that this is the timing that will work best for us."

I couldn't be bothered to talk on this subject anymore so I went to the kitchen, looked in the refrigerator, and took out some vegetables.

I didn't much like talking with my mother, so whenever I came over I always made sure to spend time in the kitchen preparing a meal. She would complain that her back hurt too much to stand in the kitchen, and as a result she was never eating properly, so her mood improved when I cooked for her. I fried some eggplant with miso, stewed some ground beef and pork I found in the freezer with daikon radish, and made some miso soup. "Too many vegetables!" she grumbled, but still she came to the table and obediently started eating.

I didn't feel like eating with her, so I drank tea and watched her use her crooked teeth to chew the food I'd cooked for her.

Whenever I was here, I always felt like I'd gone back in time to when I was young and to the little walled garden that my mother had made around us. I couldn't wait to leave her red-furnished apartment and return to the normal world I lived in.

As always her bookcase was full of old books, as though time had stood still. Did she even understand that my husband and I were going to use artificial insemination to have a child? I had the distinct impression she believed we would conceive a child by copulating, as she had, and I felt repulsed.

"This isn't enough. Make some more, will you?"

That's what she always said. I could see half-chewed rice beginning to disintegrate in her mouth.

I sometimes thought that my mother was desperate to ingest the abnormal world she believed in, the world in which man and wife committed incest and copulated. The old books and movies she had collected were no longer enough to sustain this world she so desired, so she was trying to ingest it from me and my husband. That's what I thought.

"I said it's not enough," she repeated, thinking I hadn't heard, spraying bits of rice from her mouth.

I averted my eyes and headed back into the kitchen, suppressing the urge to vomit.

I always left for work earlier than my husband, so we ate breakfast separately. I had something quick and easy, toast and scrambled egg, grabbed the bento I'd got up early to make, and headed out to my office in Nihonbashi.

It was about five minutes by train from our home in Higashi Nihonbashi. It was close enough to walk, but I always ended up taking the train.

We always started the workday with the morning assembly. I didn't want to be warned about looking too sloppy, so I enthusiastically joined in reciting the company motto, which I'd memorized, and made sure to look earnest as I listened intently to the three-minute speech given by the staff member whose turn it was that day, followed by some words from a manager, then put on a serious expression as the assembly came to an end and we got down to work. My section manager was the one in charge of the speeches today, so I kept my back even straighter.

The work I was given that morning consisted of straightforward, easy tasks, and I calmly got on with drawing up documents. I liked simple work best, but time felt as though it was passing slowly. By the time lunch break came around at last, my back was sore from sitting for so long.

It was a small company, and we were not allowed to eat lunch at our desks, so I generally joined some of the women from the section next to me in the largest meeting room, where we sat in a circle to eat our bentos. I couldn't feel very relaxed with them, though, so I often went out for lunch with Ami, a younger coworker I got along well with. But today was just before payday and we were both broke, so we joined our colleagues in the meeting room. There were eight of us today.

"Excuse me, but I have to call home," one woman said abruptly, and stood up. "It seems my kid just came down with a fever. My mother's looking after him, but he wants to hear Mama's voice."

"Oh, no! Children do get fevers often, don't they? We're not so busy today, so you can go home early if you like."

"Thank you! I think it's probably okay, but . . ."

We watched her hurry out of the room holding her phone, then looked at each other and sighed.

"It must be hard with a baby," Ami said. "And it's so difficult to take time off for childcare in this company."

"We have time allocated for morning assembly, so they should offer time for childcare too," I agreed.

Everyone nodded.

"It's apparently better than it used to be, but still. And come to think of it, you want to have a child too, don't you Amane?" a colleague my age asked.

With the conversation suddenly centered on me, I quickly nodded. "Yes, I do. In my case, my husband is planning to do the childcare, but there's no getting around the fact that I'll be the one who has to take maternity leave . . . I'll be able to transfer to a different department next year, so I'm planning to start artificial insemination after that."

"Oh really? But you'll be able to come back to work after your maternity leave, won't you? I hope your husband's company takes care of their employees better. Seriously, wouldn't it be great if men could give birth as well?" the colleague said, sounding fed up.

"I heard they've had a few cases of successful male insemination in Experiment City," Ami said, looking up from her convenience store salad. "I don't think it'll be long before men giving birth actually becomes a reality."

The woman shrugged. "Sure, but that's a government-funded project, isn't it? Even if they succeed, it won't be covered by health insurance for the rest of us, so we'll have to pay a fortune to try it. It's bound to be quite some time before it's available to everyone."

These days, most people got married for practical reasons, such as wanting children, supporting each other financially, having someone to take care of household chores so you could focus on work, and so forth. Of course, some people got married simply because they wanted a life partner, but more and more felt that it was simply preferable to live with a friend.

The so-called family system was still used when it served a purpose in life, but not when it wasn't needed. This was becoming the normal way of feeling about the system.

Based on what I saw around me, I had the impression that the percentage of people getting married was steadily decreasing. I had heard it reported on the news the other day that only 35 percent of people in their thirties were now married.

"I don't want to have kids, so I don't plan on getting married, but I'm wondering, are there any other advantages to it?" my colleague asked me innocently.

"Umm, well," I said hesitantly. "I guess having someone else at home kind of, well, there are all sorts of benefits psychologically. It's like having an absolute ally in life . . . I think there are advantages to it, myself."

"But if that's all there is to it," Ami said, leaning forward, "wouldn't it be better to share an apartment with a friend? Two women can understand each other better, for one thing."

The young woman sitting next to her pursed her lips. "No, having a family is better, you know. It's different from having a friend. Life changes when you have a true partner you can trust."

"Seriously? But surely you don't need to let a stranger into your home just so you can have kids or for financial security or whatever?"

"I don't want kids, but I'm still looking for a partner. I want to have someone with whom I am properly bound by law."

The other woman laughed at this exchange. "Sure, but I'd prefer to be able to marry a friend, then. I wish they'd just allow same-sex marriage."

"Yes, that's what I think too," said Ami, nodding vigorously. "I often talk about that with a friend who I'd love to marry if same-sex marriage was legal!"

Listening to them all, I felt like my mother had placed a curse on me.

In her red home, marriage was something that two people did when they loved each other, and becoming a family was always a wonderful thing. That's what she'd kept telling me ever since I'd been in kindergarten. I sometimes wondered whether I'd only married someone of the opposite sex because I was still tied to that notion and couldn't think freely like other people did.

"Amane, you met your husband at a matchmaking party, didn't you? I've been going to some of those too, but I don't know. I want to have a child, but I don't earn enough at this job to bring one up alone, so I need a partner. But what sort of criteria should I base my choice on? How did you choose? Amane, you want a baby, don't you? So maybe one of your criteria was the quality of his sperm, for example?" She leaned closer to me.

It seemed these days both parties sometimes showed each other the medical data for their eggs and sperm before deciding whether to get married. Just being able to live comfortably together was not enough of a deciding factor for them; having scientific information made it easier for them to narrow things down. That was hardly any different from using a sperm bank, I thought, and it didn't make much sense to me.

"No, I guess we somehow kind of hit it off."

"What? Is that all?

"Yeah . . ." I said, at a loss for words. I smiled wryly. "I don't really understand it myself. But how about you, why do you want a baby so much?" At moments like this I tended to respond by throwing the same question back at the person who asked me, thinking I may well have the same reasoning as them.

"For security, when I get old," the young woman answered without missing a beat.

"Oh, but you can't count on children nowadays, you know!" the oldest woman among us said mockingly. Her child was already in elementary school. She was probably fed up with listening to us childless women going on and on about the subject.

"Why did you have a child, then?" I asked her.

She shrugged. "I hadn't planned on having a child until I was thirty, but before that, I already felt I had too much time on my hands. I wasn't all that keen on my job, and I wanted to make something out of my life, that sort of thing. And of course, once my child was born, I realized how great it was—it's quite different having a child that carries your blood."

"Really?"

"Yes, really. Once you have a child of your own, Amane, you'll understand what I mean. No question about it."

She put a plastic forkful of the pasta she'd bought at the convenience store into her mouth.

What would they say if I told them right now that actually I'd been conceived through copulation? Everyone knew very well that it had been normal in the past. But we were different creatures now from what we were then.

I thought back vaguely to the red house where I grew up. And I thought about the world before, where the values permeating that house prevailed throughout the world. It felt a bit creepy to me, but the idea was familiar—after all, we were still now all locked in a room controlled by a particular set of values.

I squashed a tomato with my fork, and a pale red color spurted out inside the bento box.

The following weekend, my husband left home in the morning to go out on a date.

I'd decided to stay home and was cleaning the spare room.

This room would be our future child's bedroom, but for now it was a storeroom. I was piling up old magazines and clothes we no longer wore and tying them together to put them out for recycling.

When I took the magazines downstairs to the apartment building's garbage collection area, I found a bundle of old children's stories. *Dot and Anton, The Snow Queen, The Nutcracker* . . . and especially the St Clare's series that I'd loved so much.

Feeling a wave of nostalgia, I picked them up and was busy looking at the covers when I heard a voice behind me.

"Oh, would you like to have those?"

I turned to see a deeply tanned man dressed sloppily in a T-shirt and shorts standing there.

"No, no, they just took me back to my childhood a bit . . . Sorry!" I said, hastily putting them down.

The man scrunched up his face in a smile. "Have you read them? I used to read them a lot when I was a kid. That makes me feel happy."

"You read this series?" I blurted out without thinking. It was a story about a girls' boarding school, not the sort of thing you'd expect a man to have read.

"Ah, I guess not many guys have read it, huh? I might look big and strong now, but I was a real weakling as a kid and was always in and out of the hospital. Long stays in the hospital were boring, so I used to read these books and play at imagining that I was at boarding school instead."

"Wow, amazing! I loved it too. Especially the midnight feasts."

He smiled. "Wonderful! Yes, I loved those parts too. There was all sorts of food I'd never heard of, and I really wanted to try everything!"

"Are you throwing them out?"

The man looked uncomfortable. "We don't have space for them anymore. We only have a small apartment. But they bring back memories of when I was a kid, so I couldn't resist coming back down to take one last look at them. And I was surprised to find that someone else had got here first and was staring at them!"

"I'm sorry, I shouldn't have—" I said, ashamed of myself.

"What? No way! Don't apologize! I'm super happy. I really cherish those books and would much rather have someone else read them than just throw them away. That's why I asked if you wanted them, even though it was a bit cheeky of me. I'm the one who should be apologizing." He bowed his head in a small apology.

"Okay, then maybe I'll take you at your word and take them home with me. Are you sure it's okay? Seeing them here makes me want to read them again."

"Really? Yay, I'm so happy!"

"I'll give you something in return. What apartment do you live in?"

He shook his head. "No need. I'd already thrown them out anyway, so you really don't have to give me anything for them. I should be the one thanking you!" Then he added hastily, "Oh, but I hope you don't think I'm just some pickup artist. I'm in apartment 504, just so you know there's nothing suspicious about me."

"There's nothing suspicious about me either. I'm in apartment 601."

"Oh, on the sixth floor. Where that cat lives? There's a cat with '605' written on its collar that often comes onto our balcony."

"The cute white one? Yes, it comes to ours too."

"Yes, that one. It must be visiting everyone in the building!" He laughed again. He sure did laugh a lot. "I'm sorry, just imagining it makes me laugh. Look, why don't I help you carry these up to your apartment? They're pretty heavy."

He picked the books up. His arms were muscular, and I could make out his well-defined chest muscles through his T-shirt.

"So many books!" my husband exclaimed happily when he came home from his date that night. "It's like in the movies! So what was he like? Do you fancy him?"

"Not at all! I mean, he's all muscles, like he does lots of sports. Nothing like my usual type."

"We'll see. You always say that when you first meet someone you end up falling in love with, Amane."

My husband liked listening to me talk about my love life, and he seemed to want me to fall in love again. He was a bit like a little sister in that respect.

"You like hearing about my love life, don't you?" I asked him.

"Yes, because it's always simple and happy. You know how if you're feeling down it's always nice to watch a stupid romance movie with a happy ending? It's a bit like that."

"Hey, who are you calling stupid?" I nudged him with my elbow to show I was teasing him, then peered into his face and asked quietly, "Are you feeling okay?" His cheeks looked hollow.

"Yeah, I'm okay. It's just that I had a fight with my girlfriend yesterday."

"Did something bad happen?"

"No, nothing. But we still fight. However much we love each other, she's not enough for me, and I'm not enough for her, and both of us become emotional. That always happens when I fall in love. Maybe there's something in me that always jams the cogs of love."

"Ah . . ."

"I know that about myself, and yet I still fall in love again. I thought it'd be different this time, but here we are again, it always ends in tears. Even though we love each other. Why is that?"

"Hmm, I wonder. I always find loving a real person is a lot easier than loving someone from the other world. We can touch, we can talk, and I don't have that feeling of being starved when I'm in love with a real person."

"You see, that's why I like hearing about your love life, Amane. It's always joyful, with a happy ending," he said with a little smile.

"It's okay," I said, stroking his head. "As long as you are honest with each other about your feelings, the relationship will settle down eventually."

"I'm so glad I married you, Amane. To be honest, I didn't really know what it meant to become a family. I just thought you started living with some stranger, and even though you called them your family, in reality it was just something mutually convenient. But with you, Amane, I feel we are alive together."

"True. I feel the same way. At least while I'm at home I can just forget all about love and relax."

"Thank you," he said, and smiled. "The outside world is soiled by my feelings of love and my sexual appetite. The only place I feel clean is at home."

My husband's girlfriend lived alone. Maybe she didn't intend to have children. Lately, many people who didn't specifically want to have children didn't marry, finding it more comfortable to either share an apartment with someone they got along well with or live alone.

I wondered whether to mediate between my husband and his girlfriend, but it would probably be irritating to have a family member poking their nose into their relationship. All I could do was to listen when my husband wanted to talk about it.

"Are you hungry? I didn't have much to do today, so I made cassoulet. And also some ratatouille to eat chilled."

My husband and I both liked stews. My husband did the cooking during the week, but on weekends when he didn't have a date we made stew together or took turns in the kitchen, working together to make a feast.

Cleaning was my domain, and on the weekend I did all the laundry at once and then put it in the dryer. Since I didn't clean every day, I felt that my husband had the heavier burden of housework, so now and then when I had time, I would treat him to some homemade food when he came home tired from a date.

We had separate bedrooms, but on those days when we cooked together, we would curl up with each other like cats on the sofa to sleep.

I smiled at him as I heated up the cassoulet. "Being at home is reassuring, isn't it? We're too busy with love when we're out."

My husband looked almost euphoric somehow. "Yes, you're right."

"I've heard that falling in love is basically just entertainment for our lower bodies. And it's true, isn't it? Naturally the most important thing in life is family."

"Yes, that's right. Obviously."

As if making fun of ourselves for being slaves to that lower-body entertainment, we laughed and kept talking, repeating the word "family."

"When I think about family, I feel at peace. Knowing I have a family, I feel calm regardless of whatever happens outside."

"And we'll have a child sometime too. I'm looking forward to that. We'll be so busy with family that we won't have time to waste on things like love affairs."

"That's right. And we'll be bringing up a new life that has inherited our genes. I'm really looking forward to our family growing."

Having been made to suffer by the religion of romantic love, we wanted to be saved by the religion of family. If we could succeed in truly brainwashing our entire bodies, I had the feeling we could finally forget romantic love.

"Raising a new life is the most important life work of all. I'm so glad I made a family."

Laughing, we served up the warm cassoulet and sat down at the dining table.

Every time I said the word "family," I had the feeling I was saying a prayer. This really was a religion, I thought. Every time we said that word, we became even more faithful believers.

Now that the conversation had turned to family, my husband started to look a bit better. His family with me and our future child was saving him from the love outside the home that was making him suffer. That was beautiful, I thought, feeling elated.

We had entered into a marriage contract because we were useful to each other in terms of raising a child. However, my husband was not just a stranger acting as a sperm donor. He was family.

The thought that we were properly integrated within the system was a relief. We weren't just using the family system because it was useful; it also gave rise to a kind of unshakable bond.

Love and sexual desire were like waste material, something to be disposed of outside the home. But on nights when we suffered spasms of loneliness, we could cuddle and enjoy talking together. Sometimes we would spew out what was festering in our minds, and other times we would just chat about nothing in particular.

This was how we confirmed our closeness to each other's lives and felt reassured. It was also like we were desperately trying to convince ourselves that we did at least have one absolute ally in life, called "family." We would live together our whole lives, sharing the pain of this spasm called love.

We kept talking about family as if to make ourselves believe in it.

"I want to put the baby's crib in my bedroom, so we'll only start using the baby's room after some time."

"We're only planning on having one child, but if it's really cute, I might end up wanting another one too. If so, this apartment will be too small."

"Let's move to the suburbs if we can save up enough. It's better for children to play somewhere surrounded by nature."

"I wonder whether it'll be a boy or a girl."

"I don't mind either way. Our child is going to be really cute, whichever it is."

I would take maternity leave to give birth, after which my husband would take childcare leave until the child was three years old. My husband's company had better employee benefits, and it would be easier for him to go back to work after parental leave.

"I wish I could give birth, though," he said. "Then I could take maternity and childcare leave, and you wouldn't have to take any time off work at all, Amane."

"Absolutely. I wonder how those experimental artificial wombs are coming along?"

"The technology is really hard to get right. Apparently, it'd be easier to use an animal's womb."

"Hmm."

Maybe the time would come when my eggs would be fertilized by my husband's sperm and implanted in the womb of an animal, and our baby would be taken out of a pig or a cow. There wouldn't be any need for a person to have a womb anymore, I thought idly.

"I feel more cheerful when we talk about our child."

"A new life is like another light coming on in the home, they say. That's the meaning of family."

"Isn't it wonderful? Keeping life going like that."

After dinner we had dessert and then slept together on the sofa. My husband's body warmth was like that of a pet cat or dog. We cared for each other's body warmth in our daily lives as though it were a beloved pet. Reassured by this thought, I fell asleep.

The next day I took an earlier train than usual to work.

Today it was my turn to give the speech at morning assembly, but the manager told me off for not being concise enough and I felt frazzled from anxiety and stress.

I picked up my bag and went to the bathroom, where I took out my Prada pouch and gazed at my forty lovers inside.

The small buttons, key chains, magazine cuttings, and so forth stuffed inside had all the characters I had loved: the seven-thousand-year-old immortal boy warrior, the boy detective who received secret orders from the police, the UFO pilot, the newborn android who couldn't control his own strength, the prince who rode a dragon into battle . . . After gazing at them for a while and watching a video of Krom on my phone, I started to feel better.

I felt them all cheering me on as I left the bathroom and went back to my desk, and I was able to concentrate on my work. I even managed to complete a particularly tricky document before noon without making any mistakes.

At lunchtime, my younger coworker Ami invited me to go out to lunch, just the two of us.

I really didn't want to see my manager, so I quickly agreed.

We went to a soba restaurant some distance from the office.

"I got a really bad telling-off by my leader this morning," Ami said, and sighed. "Makes me want to leave this job."

"Yeah, I know how you feel. He doesn't mince his words, does he? He was in a really bad mood this morning. I heard he had a big argument with the section head after the morning assembly. Just put it down to bad luck. It's not worth worrying about."

Ami didn't look any happier, and didn't have any appetite either.

"Just getting through the day can be tough. I spent the whole morning thinking about *Blue Sniper*, like how yesterday's battle was really cool, how great the new opening sequence is, that sort of thing. That helps, for some reason. It really gives me the energy to carry on living," she said, sighing, talking about a popular animation.

"I couldn't agree more," I said. "It gives me the strength to go on. Some people say it's escaping reality, but I don't agree. Rather, it's nourishing my soul so that I can live in reality."

"What?" Ami looked at me in surprise. "But you have a husband, Amane. I thought having a family was the source of strength for people."

"Well yes, but . . ."

"But you still get your strength from anime characters? So what is family to you, Amane?"

"Family is different. Of course it's what is closest to me and gives me the most support. But I also respect the people from all the stories I've ever loved, and they are super important to me too," I said, feeling a bit flustered and getting tongue-tied. It was true, my husband did give me energy to live. After all, he was my family.

"Of course, you have a family, Amane, so I think my situation is a bit different, but the characters I like really do give me the strength to live. I would probably die if I didn't have them. Life is too difficult! If there wasn't anywhere at all to let my soul take a break, I would probably just collapse."

She stopped talking, then suddenly gave me a strange look. "But Amane, you have real people for lovers too, don't you? Like, you go both ways? That's pretty unusual these days."

"I guess. Although quite a few people around me do the same thing."

"I suppose real-life lovers have sex?"

"Well, it depends," I answered with a wry smile. She hadn't meant any harm, and didn't seem all that interested in my answer.

"I'm so conflicted," she said, talking about herself again. "I love my favorite characters, but—and maybe I shouldn't tell you this—but I use them for sexual relief."

"Sexual relief . . . Oh, you don't need to put it like that. And I don't think it's so terrible."

"But sometimes I suddenly come to my senses and realize I'm defiling the person I love most. They're supposed to be sacred, but I use them for masturbation. I rape what I cherish the most!"

"No, it's natural, because you love them. When you fall in love with someone in a story, you want to connect your bodies. It's an emotion that comes from a pure place. You love them so much that your flesh responds. There's nothing dirty about it."

"I don't know . . . I'm doing something really vulgar to them. Is it okay to sugarcoat that with words like 'love' and 'romance'?"

I choked up at this and couldn't answer. I remembered how, back in school, Mizuuchi and Juri had looked uncomfortable and told me that what I was doing was just masturbation when I'd insisted that I'd been having sex with Lapis.

I had always felt that what we were doing was sex, and that we loved each other. But maybe that had just been my sugarcoating and I'd actually been raping them like Ami said.

"I'm sorry," Ami said brightly, seeing me go quiet. "I shouldn't be saying these things to you, Amane. I didn't invite you out to lunch to sit here complaining about this sort of thing! Anyway, I've been thinking about things lately and have decided to leave my job."

"What?" I looked at her in surprise.

"Oh, not right away, of course," she added. "But I want to have a baby. I've always wanted to, and I've been saving up. I mean, even if I take childcare leave from this job, it'll be hard to come back to work here afterward. So I've been saving up enough money to live on between leaving work and the child entering kindergarten, and then I'll look for another job."

"Oh . . ."

"But I haven't even decided which hospital to go to for artificial insemination yet, so it won't be any time soon," she said with a smile.

"Haven't you thought about getting a partner? It'll be hard to save up enough on your own, won't it?"

Ami grimaced. "Well, yes, I did consider it, but . . . I really don't like the idea of having a stranger in my home. A child I gave birth to myself is one thing, but my home will be cleaner without a complete stranger living there. Oh, I'm sorry, Amane. I don't mean to judge your choice. It's just that personally I could never do it. So I'm really glad I have a womb. I have this possibility."

"I see . . ." I did my best to say something, but I couldn't eat much after that.

I'm glad I have a womb. That was what stuck in my ears. If my husband had a womb, would he still have chosen to live with me? Was the fact I had a womb the only reason he called me family?

I must have been hungry, but I couldn't finish my tempura soba and left more than half uneaten.

Ami didn't notice, though, and just kept chatting about her favorite anime characters.

I tried to imagine her raising a child in her clean world, but it was hazy, and I couldn't quite visualize a baby in my mind.

I'd told hardly anyone since elementary school about having been conceived through copulation. I hadn't even told my husband.

Juri was the only one I'd confessed it to.

That had been back in high school. Our exhibition had just ended, and the two of us were alone in the classroom. Juri was assiduously getting on with painting, but I put a teabag in a mug, poured on water from the hot water pot, and sat there drinking it.

"If you're not going to paint, just go home, will you? I'll lock up," she said, sounding irritated.

"Hmm, maybe later," I answered, and carried on gazing out the window.

"What's up?" she asked. "Is there something you want to talk about?"

I looked down. "Not particularly . . ." I said in a small voice. "Juri, what sort of people are your mom and dad?"

"Very ordinary. Dad is busy with work and not at home much. Mom's a typical housewife. Every now and then they invite their lovers around for a party, though. It's a bit of a pain, really."

"Really? So they all get along well, then?"

"Both Mom and Dad have been going out with their lovers for a long time. Dad's girlfriend is about the same age as Mom, and they're good friends—like, they even go away on trips together sometimes. Not that I'm interested. Love is just entertainment, that's what I think, anyway."

"Um . . . I was conceived when my mom and dad copulated."

"Huh?"

"Do you think that's gross? They deliberately went to the hospital to get the contraceptive devices removed, then copulated as a married couple, and later Mom gave birth to me. Dad left us before I was old enough to understand, but I still feel grossed out by the thought that he committed incest with Mom. There are photos of him at home, but I try not to look at them."

"Ah."

"I sometimes wonder whether Mom is trying to put a curse on me. I fall in love with real people too, right? When I was little, Mom showed me a lot of old books, and made me believe that someday I would get married, commit incest with the person I'd become family with, and have a baby with that person. Later on I learned about the right way, but it's like I've been left with this curse on my body."

Juri sat painting with her back ramrod straight for a few moments. Then she said, "What are you going on about? This hasn't got anything to do with anything. You are you, here and now, that's all that matters. And what's right today isn't what was right a hundred years ago. There's been a time slip from the right world of a hundred years ago to the right world now, a hundred years later. That's all."

"I don't know . . . I always feel the need to confirm that my sexual urges are different from my mother's. I'm always reassured to find out that they are. That's why whenever I fall in love, I connect our bodies. Do you think that's dirty?"

"No, I don't. Although I do think it's futile. I mean, there's no such thing as a right way to be sexually aroused."

"Yeah, maybe, but I want to be able to feel aroused with peace of mind. Every time I fall in love with a real person, I'm always horrified it might be because of Mom's curse. It keeps happening time and time again, and I'm sick of it."

"So I'm saying there's no such thing as peace of mind when it comes to sexual arousal. Humans are evolving rapidly, and our spirit and instincts are changing. There's no such thing as a perfect animal in this world, so a flawless instinct doesn't exist either. We're all animals in the process of evolving. So whether or not our instincts match the world is just a coincidence, and we have no idea what will be considered right in the next instance."

"Hmm."

"We are just a blip in evolution. We're always midway in that chain."

"I don't know . . . When will humans be perfected, then?"

"Never! Cro-Magnon man probably thought he was perfect, and the same for Australopithecus. The shape of the skull and the internal organs, the length of our arms and legs—they all keep changing. And along with that you have the soul and the brain and whatnot, which change even more quickly. The idea of rightness really is an illusion. Pursuing it is a waste of time, in my opinion," she said flatly, then added, "Anyway, stop talking nonsense. If you're not going to paint, do something useful like clean the room. Look, why don't you tidy up those cloisonné tools they were using earlier," pointing to one corner of the room.

"Slave driver!" I said, but I felt her clumsy affection for me and obediently started cleaning up.

The picture Juri was painting was a still life, with a background of graded colors moving from blue to yellow.

Was I, too, one of those changing colors? For some reason the thought made my eyeballs feel hot, and I looked down at my toes.

After that, Juri never mentioned our discussion again. Even after we grew up, got married, and started talking about children, the subject never came up again.

But now and then I would hazily recall it. The word "midway" that Juri had given me at that time was comforting on the one hand, but it had convinced me all the more that I would always have to keep confirming my own truth.

Therefore, even now, whenever I fell in love I always had to check. I had to confirm the nature of my sexual arousal now, in this moment, as if conducting an experiment.

On Saturday afternoon I rang the doorbell for apartment number 504.

I wanted to deliver a gift to the man I'd met the other day in return for the books. After giving it a lot of thought, I settled on a pack of assorted teas from a department store.

I intended to hang the bag on the doorknob if nobody was in, but the door opened immediately and the man's wife came out.

She was in the middle of putting hot curlers in her brown hair, with only one side completed.

"I'm sorry to drop by like this. I live upstairs, and the other day your husband was kind enough to let me have some books he was throwing out. This is just a small token of my gratitude."

She stared at me for a moment, but then beamed and grabbed my sleeve.

"Oh, thank you so much! I've heard all about you. He said he'd been chatting up a gorgeous woman. How amazing that you're here now! Please wait a moment. He's in his room so I'll just go get him."

His wife ran down the corridor and opened a door, and I heard her call excitedly, "Mizuhito, that woman you told me about? She's here!"

After a few moments of confused commotion, the man I'd met the other day came out, hurriedly pulling on an orange T-shirt.

"Sorry to keep you waiting!"

"Not at all, I'm the one who should be sorry. Did I wake you up, by any chance?"

He looked flustered, and his hair was tousled. He looked even younger than he had the other day.

"No, it's already past noon. I drank a bit too much yesterday . . . I was still in bed in my underwear." He laughed, looking a little embarrassed, and I almost burst out laughing myself.

"I'm sorry to barge in on you like this. I just wanted to thank you for giving me so many books. I've been enjoying reading them."

"Oh, there's no need. But I'm happy you came. Ah, I love coffee, that's great."

"Oh, sorry, it's tea, actually."

He peered into the bag sheepishly. "Oh, but I like tea too. But what am I saying? I was really hoping I'd see you again. I was wondering how come we never run into our neighbors in this building."

His wife came out into the hallway still fixing her hair.

"All you have to do is say how happy you are to see her!" She turned to me. "Ever since he met you, he's been going on about how lovely you are. He's been going to throw out the garbage every day on the off chance of running into you again. He's like a schoolboy; it makes me laugh," she said, patting him on the back.

"Oh, do be quiet. Hurry up and go out. Your boyfriend's waiting for you!"

"Okay, okay! Well, I'm headed out, so please make yourself at home."

She took some high-heeled shoes out of the shoe cupboard, slipped her feet into them, bowed to me, and left.

"I'm sorry, my wife can be far too familiar."

"Not at all, she's lovely. Is she going out on a date now?"

"Yes, she is. She's just started going out with some young guy. She's so excited, that's why she's started teasing me. I mean really! You saw her, right? Dressed up in a miniskirt. Because he's young, you see. She's the one who's on a high!"

Seeing him babbling away, trying to cover up for his flushed cheeks, I started feeling shy and didn't know what to say anymore.

His collarbone was peeping out of his orange T-shirt. What a beautiful shape that bone is, I thought, and felt something start wriggling inside me.

"Is this one lemon tea? Wow, it smells great," he said, opening a can and sniffing the contents.

I moved closer to him and stumbled.

"Hey, are you okay?" he asked, hastily holding me up.

I clung onto the hem of his T-shirt, which was permeated with his body heat. Oh, my body's talking, I thought. *More!* the voice came from within me. *I want to touch him! I want to take in his body heat!*

At this point, I was probably already head over heels in love with him.

"Let me treat you to dinner to say thanks," he said.

"What? I'm supposed to be the one thanking you!"

"Well then, how about we go up to the roof?" he suggested. "Have you ever been up there?"

"Never. There's a fence barrier, isn't there?"

"I go up from time to time. It's easy enough to get over the fence. The weather's nice, so how about having a picnic up there? I just happen to have some wine and sandwiches."

"That sounds wonderful. I'd love to," I said. A picnic on the roof sounded so charming that I accepted his offer without a second thought.

I carried the sandwiches and cheese while he brought some glasses and a bottle of chilled white wine, and together we climbed up the stairs to the roof.

Our apartment block was eleven stories high. As he'd said, when we reached the top there was a fence with a small NO ENTRY sign. We climbed over this and had the big, wide roof space to ourselves.

"I sometimes come here to drink beer and gaze at the view of the city at night. It feels so good! There's such a great view."

"It's wonderful. Funny to think that I've never been here before, even though I live in this building."

We laid out the sandwiches and cheese and toasted each other with white wine.

"Wow, it's sweet!" The wine he'd brought was actually a bit too sweet. "Mizuhito, wasn't it?"

"Huh?"

"Your name. It just occurred to me that I hadn't asked you yet. I heard your wife call you that earlier."

"No, actually it's Mizuto. It's written with the characters for 'water' and 'person,' 'mizu' and 'hito,' and my wife always ends up saying Mizuhito."

"Mizuto. Nice name."

"What about you?"

"Amane, with the characters for 'rain' and 'sound.' "

"So we both have water names!" He laughed happily.

Eating one of the sandwiches his wife had made, I said, "You weren't throwing away books so much as getting rid of a former girlfriend, weren't you?"

"What?"

"I realized that while I was reading them. You were in love with a girl in one of those books, weren't you?"

"I had too many girlfriends," he said awkwardly, "so I decided to tidy up a bit. I kept six and threw the rest out."

"I see."

"But then . . . I got another one." He awkwardly touched the ends of my hair briefly.

Before he could withdraw his hand, I grabbed it and gave it a squeeze. He looked taken aback, but when I squeezed harder without saying anything, his shoulders relaxed.

"The veins really stand out on the back of your hand, don't they, Mizuto?" I said, apropos of nothing, feeling shy.

"Yep. They stand out even more on my arms."

He also seemed a little shy, and still holding my hand raised his other arm to show me. Blue veins stood out against his suntanned skin.

"Nurses often tell me it's super easy to give me injections."

"Do you do any sports?"

"I used to play basketball and soccer, but I think my muscles are more due to my job. I do takuhai deliveries and am always carrying heavy boxes."

"I see." I wanted so badly to touch his veins, but I resisted.

"Amane, are you the sort to fall in love with real people too?" he asked, his expression serious.

"Yes, I am."

"I'm so glad!"

"What about you, Mizuto?"

"I've also fallen in love with real people several times."

"Really? Then I'm glad too! These days I hardly ever come across people who have love affairs with both real people and people from the other world, the way I do."

"The other world?"

"Oh, that's what I call people who live inside a story, because they feel so near to us yet so far. I got the phrase from a boyfriend I had during junior high."

"Hmm, it sounds quite mysterious. Reminds me of the world of the dolls in *The Nutcracker*." He laughed. "But I think loving real people is completely different from loving fictional characters. You can easily go out with more than one character at a time. With characters, it's like I'm being forced to feel a particular emotion and I get tired of that sometimes. I feel they're specifically designed to make me sexually aroused or have pseudo-romantic feelings for them. It can happen when

I'm just walking on the street or watching TV, and before I know it, I'm having money extorted out of me. I feel like I've been deceived. It's a bit like going to a hostess bar and finding some yakuza behind it."

"Really? I guess it's especially like that for men. When I was in high school, a potty-mouthed friend of mine said that characters are consumables for sexual relief. It's a horrible way of putting it, though."

"Mmm, in my case I feel more like I'm the one being consumed. It feels like before I know what's happening, I'm being dragged into this pseudo-romance system, instilling pseudo-romantic feelings in us to make us consume so that it can ultimately devour us. After all, that's how the economy works, isn't it? These are businesses to make you fall in love, and I feel like I'm being targeted. That's why I sometimes hate the system. I get it that the characters aren't to blame, though. But that's why I decided to cut down on them and was clearing them out."

"I see . . ."

Both Mizuto and Ami called nonhuman lovers "characters." I couldn't bring myself to do that, so I just nodded vaguely.

"Maybe I've drunk too much. That always happens when I drink wine."

Mizuto's cheeks were flushed. I stroked the scab on his arm.

"That looks painful."

"It doesn't bother me at all. I do physical work, so I'm always getting injured. Look, here's another one. But it doesn't hurt at all."

He rolled up his trouser leg and showed me a cut on his shin.

My husband and I hardly ever hurt ourselves, so it had been ages since I'd last seen a scab. Feeling a little nostalgic, I reached out my hand to gently touch it.

Mizuto's skin was thick and rough to the touch, and his scab was surrounded by a purple bruise like a hydrangea blossom. I had the feeling his skin was made from a different material than mine and my husband's.

"Is it fun to touch that?" He burst out laughing, seeing me look so serious as I touched his wound and the skin around it. His large eyes narrowed as he laughed, and I felt my fingertips tingle as I touched his skin.

"Mizuto, have you ever had sex?" I asked suddenly.

He shook his head, taken aback. "Never. You mean like copulation in the old days, right? I've had lovers, but we never did anything old-fashioned like that."

"I guess not."

"Wait, are you saying you have, Amane?"

"Yes, I've always done it with my lovers."

"Really? I never hear about it in my circles, so I thought nobody did it anymore."

"There are still a few of us left. Barely, though."

Mizuto held my hand. "If it's a condition for dating you, Amane, then I'll do it."

"It's not a condition as such, it's just that I've always done it."

"What does it matter whether you do it or not? Isn't it just a relic from the old days?"

"Yeah, it's just that I find it reassuring."

Now Mizuto stroked my head, sinking his fingers into my hair. They had a different kind of heat than my husband's.

Still holding hands, we went downstairs to Mizuto's apartment and sat on the sofa bed in the living room.

"Do we have to make any preparations, like with some tools or something?"

"No, it's okay. All we need are our sexual organs."

I took off my skirt and knickers and Mizuto took off his jeans and boxers, and we sat facing each other.

"So now we have to stimulate our brains. Then our sexual organs will naturally get ready."

"Got it."

Sitting there naked from the waist down, we each looked at sexual images and movies on our cell phones to prepare our own sexual organs. I watched a movie of my lover Krom.

"How do you know when your sexual organ is ready?"

"The evidence is water coming out of a woman and a man's penis getting hard."

"Let me try."

For a while we sat in silence, staring at our phones, and when I felt I was ready I said, "I think I'm okay now."

"Yeah, me too, I think. What do we do now?"

"You have to put that into something called the vaginal

opening. I don't think you can find it by yourself, so I'll show you." I opened my legs and pointed to my vagina.

"I can't really see any opening . . . Is that okay?"

"It's made from quite an elastic material, so it's okay."

"Weird. Did people in the old days really do this?"

"Everyone did, apparently. I mean, this is how humans are designed to copulate."

"Very strange."

Mizuto looked totally mystified as he pushed his penis against my groin.

"Now you have to move your hips to stimulate our sexual organs. Then some liquid will come out of your sexual organ, Mizuto, and when that happens, it's over."

"Sounds difficult! I'll do my best."

By trial and error we stimulated our sexual organs, and eventually some liquid came out of Mizuto.

The inside of my vagina was dry, and I felt a sharp pain that I'd never felt before. The sensation of water flowing into my body was much more mysterious than usual. It felt like Mizuto was making it rain inside my body.

When Mizuto took his sexual organ out of me, liquid made clear by his contraceptive device flowed smoothly out, just as it had from Mizuuchi back in junior high.

"This is sperm, isn't it?" Mizuto said, touching the drops of clear liquid on my thighs. "I've ejected this before too."

"Did it make your body quiet?"

"What?"

"That's what the boy said the first time I had sex—that his body went quiet once this liquid came out. Come to think of it, his name was Mizuuchi, written with the character for 'water' just like your name, Mizuto."

"Really? You do have a connection with water, don't you, Amane? But in my case, I don't go quiet. Rather, my body gets more agitated." He buried his face in my shirt.

"Sex is somehow like a ritual, isn't it? I wonder if other animals feel like this when they copulate?" I touched Mizuto's spine through his orange T-shirt. "Mizuto, your bones and your veins are beautiful."

"Bones?"

"Your skin makes the shape of your bones stand out. It's so beautiful."

Mizuto narrowed his eyes in a smile. "Nobody's said anything like that to me before. You're complimenting my bones and veins, of all things! Even though they're inside my skin."

"Appreciating what's under the skin is what love is all about, isn't it?"

"I guess. Yes, probably."

I ran my fingers along the veins standing out in the dark skin on his neck.

"For some reason, I'm really tired. Maybe it's from carrying out the ritual."

"Go ahead and sleep."

"I kind of feel like a sacrificial victim." He closed his eyes.

"Yes, I understand. I think it is like a ritual."

I touched my lips to Mizuto's forehead. He fell asleep, snoring regularly. Even when I moved away, his body heat was still left on the palm of my hand.

Every time I had sex with a real person, I had a dream from my childhood.

Just as I had once believed what my mother had instilled in me in that red house, I now couldn't break this habit of putting my lover's sexual organ inside my body. Like a child sucking its thumb, I devoured my partner's body with my mucous membrane.

I wanted to howl that what I was doing was nothing like the copulation between my mother and father, just a ritual done only for love, but the howl stayed inside, clawing at my chest. Outside the window it was gray, a gray that to my eyes had a tinge of red.

To escape it, I looked away and buried my face in Mizuto's T-shirt as he slept.

"Wow, you're in love again for real!"

The next day, Sunday, I told my husband about it as we made some zuppa forte that a local Italian bar had given me a recipe for.

"It's wonderful that your new boyfriend lives in the same building," he said. "You can meet him whenever you want!"

"Well, yes, but it also means that I can't just pop down to get a newspaper without looking my best anymore. I even have to dress up to go throw away the garbage!"

"Ah, that's a drag. But still, I'm envious."

I was beginning to feel a bit embarrassed about my husband's interest in my love affair. "Hey, time to add the tomato and stock," I said, tapping him on the back.

"Now it just has to simmer for four or five hours, right?"

"Let's hope it tastes good!"

We turned down the heat under the pan and sat down on the sofa together to drink some barley tea.

"I'm thirsty. Do you fancy a beer, Amane?"

"Mmm, not really. I'd like to have some chilled wine with the food when it's ready. I'll wait for that."

"Oh, okay, I'll go ahead and have one now anyway."

My husband brought a beer for himself, poured it into a glass, and put a slice of lemon in it.

"What's that, lemon and beer?! Does it taste good?"

"Yes, I do it when I want a refreshing drink. It's not exactly like a Corona with lime, but it's pretty good."

"Can I have a sip?"

"Ha, that's why I asked you if you wanted some!" he said with a wry smile, passing me the glass.

I was thirsty after cooking, and it was so refreshing that I ended up going to get another glass with some lemon slices and started drinking with him.

"How are things going with your girlfriend, Saku?" I asked casually.

His face darkened. "Not too good," he said, and smiled weakly. "That's why I want to hear about your affair, Amane. I only want to hear blissful stories headed for a happy ending."

I hoped my husband's love affair would go well too. He was like a little sister I had to keep an eye on. He wanted to innocently listen to me talk about my love affair, while the pain of his own love affair was tearing his heart to shreds.

"But why does it hurt so much if you both love each other?"

"It's always the same with my love affairs. The more I put into it, the more it's not enough, and it gets painful. I start getting creaky inside, and my love gears get out of whack. Maybe it's my nature. You always seem so happy, Amane."

"But I really wish you could be happy in love, Saku. You're family, and really important to me."

"Thank you."

He leaned his head on my shoulder as though drained of energy.

His hair felt like the feathers on a little bird, and having his head on my shoulder felt like having a bird perched there.

I had never so much as touched his skin, so whenever I thought of him, it was the sensation of his soft hair that came to mind. His body heat, like an innocent pet's, could be felt through his hair.

"Saku, you only ever fall in love with real people, don't you? And you also have sex with your lovers. Why is that, I wonder?"

"Why are you asking all of a sudden?"

"Because hardly anyone does that anymore, do they? Even when I fall in love with someone, I kind of take it for granted they'll never have had sex before."

"I guess not. When I was about twenty, I fell head over heels for a girl and I wanted to know everything about her, so I tried it after reading about it in books. It felt like a kind of ritual to make her mine. But in the end it only led to pain."

"When I was in elementary school, I tried it because I thought that's what you did when you fell in love. It was fun, and I was happy. So I always do it whenever I get a new lover too."

"Me too, I always do it when I'm really in love. It's like I'm praying that the ritual will work this time."

"We're the opposite of Adam and Eve."

"What the heck?" He laughed.

Relieved, I went on, "Well, Adam and Eve ate the forbidden fruit and came to know shame and love, didn't they? So now everyone's eating the fruit that's the antidote to the forbidden fruit, and they are all returning to paradise. I think we might end up being the last ones left behind."

"Well, that's a bit scary. I don't suppose sex is a ritual to achieve love in paradise, is it?"

"In paradise, there probably isn't any sex."

"Yeah, I think you're right. Sex is rapidly disappearing from the world. In fifty years, the only people still having sex will probably be us and our lovers."

"Are you scared?"

"Not as long as I'm with you, Amane. After all, we're family."

He snuggled his soft hair up to me as if he were an exhausted cat.

For a while we chatted and watched a silly film on satellite TV until the zuppa forte was ready, then we toasted each other with wine and started dinner.

We'd left the TV on, and images from Experiment City in Chiba Prefecture were shown as the local news came on.

"If we're the opposite of Adam and Eve, maybe that's the paradise that humankind is returning to?" my husband murmured.

The TV presenter was repeating the same old information that I'd become sick of hearing.

> It will soon be ten years since Chiba was reborn as Experiment City. There is a celebratory mood, and events are being planned in various locations.
>
> As you know, Chiba Experiment City has replaced the family system with a new system for raising children and continuing life, based on comprehensive research from the fields of psychology and biology.

Once a year, on December 24, residents selected at random by computer algorithms are artificially inseminated en masse. The whole population is managed by computers, and eligibility for selection is based on health and past childbirth records. By tightly controlling the number of children born every year, the population is maintained at an optimum level with no significant increase or decrease.

Selected men are fitted with an artificial womb and inseminated. None of these male artificial wombs succeeded fully this year either, but implants into the uterine lining were successful in five hundred cases, and four of those managed to grow the fetus for several months inside the womb. Hopes are building that a man will successfully give birth for the first time next year.

The children born under the artificial insemination program are raised from birth by the Center. All are guaranteed food, clothing, and shelter at the Center until they come of age, when as adults they themselves are able to receive artificial insemination and leave the Center.

In this society, the children call all the adults "Mother." They are doted on by all the adults, who shower them with affection.

The first group of children born in the program are now eight years old. Unlike in the family system, these children are all given consistent affection and are emotionally stable, and they are demonstrably superior both intellectually and physically. They do not have to bear the unfair risk of being part of a flawed family. This paradise in which children are raised and loved equally by all adults is called the Paradise-Eden System.

It will soon be time for the children conceived by artificial insemination on December 24 to be born, the earliest in late August and then through September.

Preparations for the eleventh insemination will begin immediately. Celebratory ceremonies will be held in various locations, and dignitaries from around the world will be coming to observe.

In the not-so-distant future, all of humankind will be breeding not through the Family System but through our new Paradise-Eden System.

Tonight, we shall be broadcasting a special program about the way Experiment City is shaping the future of the human race with our cutting-edge technology, and the efforts of the researchers who have brought about its amazing successes to date.

"The concept of family doesn't exist in that world, does it? Before long the effect of the forbidden fruit will wear off and humans will end up returning to paradise," I murmured, although I didn't really believe it. "Sex aside, can society really function well without family?"

"Who knows? But it'd be amazing if they're successful." My husband was leaning forward, riveted by the news.

"That's not like you to show interest in this kind of news, Saku!"

"I mean, it's revolutionary. This is a massive human experiment! Can humans really breed in this new system where families don't exist? If it succeeds, it will be groundbreaking!" he said excitedly, then looked at me and hastily added, "But of course, society can't possibly function without family, can it? If their system works well, our whole world will cease to exist."

"Right? It can't possibly work."

"It's like a breeding factory—really creepy."

I was relieved to hear my husband speak disparagingly of Experiment City.

"Hey, how about some wine? We've still got that one that tasted disgusting—there's some leftover fruit too, so we could whip up some sangria to use everything up."

"Sounds great, let's do that."

We put some orange and kiwi and other fruits into the wine, then clinked our glasses.

We had followed the recipe for the zuppa forte to the letter, but it hadn't turned out as delicious as it had been in the restaurant.

"Maybe we put too much tomato in."

"Hmm? I think it tastes pretty good, actually. Still, if we let it simmer for longer, the flavor should deepen."

Being able to share such culinary failures was also one of the pleasures of being family. If what we knew as family vanished from the world, surely moments like these would no longer happen?

I didn't think that was possible, but they were already conducting the experiment. Already, sex, which had been so commonplace in the past, was rapidly vanishing from our world.

Feeling left behind, I averted my eyes from the TV and drank my sangria.

How had Adam and Eve spent their first night after leaving paradise?

The now-cold bread lay on the dinner table. Staring at it, I poured more wine into my empty glass.

Following the map, I finally arrived at the restaurant to find Mika and Emiko already seated at the table in a private room, studying the menu.

"Sorry I'm late, I got lost!"

"You've got no sense of direction, Amane! We were waiting for you before getting started."

"What will you have to drink, Amane?"

I hastily ordered a glass of champagne and sat down.

Mika and Emiko were classmates from high school. Together with Juri, the four of us often used to hang out together, and even now as adults we would sometimes get together for a meal.

"Where's Juri today?"

"Her baby's still so small, and she said she's too busy to come."

"Well, she does tend to act superior sometimes, so we're probably more comfortable without her," Emiko said with a shrug.

"Well yes, she's beautiful, but she's good-natured too, isn't she?" I said.

"It's not about her looks," Mika said. "Look, Juri's always so contemptuous toward those of us in love with anime characters, isn't she? She's been like that since high school. She's not a bad person, but I have a problem with that side of her."

Neither Mika nor Emiko had ever been in love with a real person, and it was the same with a lot of my friends. Not only sex but love between people seemed to be disappearing from this world.

Mika had never married, but she'd had her children young, and now her daughter was in her fifth year of elementary school, and her son would be starting elementary school next year. Emiko apparently didn't particularly want to have kids and planned to carry on living just as she was now. I had the feeling that remaining single would become the norm in the not-so-distant future. Even among us four high school friends, Juri and I were the only married ones.

"Mika, isn't it tough bringing up kids on your own?"

"Well, one of my roommates is self-employed, so I can usually ask her for help. Having three women sharing an apartment makes things pretty comfortable, you know? Way better than being married, for sure!" she said with a laugh, then, seeing my face, hurriedly added, "Oh, but from a financial point of view it must be better to live with a man, I'm sure. Anyone inclined to use the marriage system should do so, of course."

It wasn't as if my husband and I were only together out of self-interest. But insisting that was the case would just sound petty, so I laughed and said, "Three women living together sounds nice. Must be fun."

"Well, it's not always easy. But the three of us all have savings, and it's like a marriage of three women, really. It can be a struggle—for one thing, one of us is really untidy."

"Right? Without kids I can get by just fine. I'm better off on my own," Emiko said with a shrug.

More and more people were choosing different ways of living, and it was getting harder and harder to answer the question of why I'd got married. I was making it my new religion. That was the most concise way of putting it, but I didn't feel I could explain my reasoning well.

Mika and Emiko said that Juri held them in contempt, but I also sometimes felt they looked down on the two of us for being married. They were following a new way of living, and from their point of view they probably wondered why we bothered to be bound by the old system.

Once we'd generally caught up with recent developments, the conversation turned to love.

For the past year, Mika had been in love with a boy in a magical girl animation series that was on morning TV. Emiko had recently started being attracted to adult men and had fallen in love with a mysterious and powerful evil character in a popular CGI animation film series.

"What about your love life, Amane?"

"Yes, I only found out about your love affairs with real people after growing up, Amane. I was so shocked! I never knew!"

"So, are you in love with someone now? Come on, tell us!"

The image of Mizuto rose up in my mind, but I just smiled and brushed off the question. "No, not at the moment. I'm taking a little break for now."

"Seriously? That's no fun!"

The two of them immediately lost interest, and the conversation turned to how Mika's daughter had got her first period and Mika had taken her to the gynecologist to have the contraceptive device fitted.

"It's incredible how much medicine has progressed. Back in our day, it hurt quite a bit, didn't it? Now it doesn't hurt at all, apparently. And it was all over so quickly, only about ten minutes. Amazing!"

"Wow, that's great!"

"And it's more effective than before too. Now they hardly ever get their period. Kids these days are so lucky! I'm thinking of having one of the new devices fitted myself. My period's so heavy every month."

"But it's really expensive if the insurance doesn't cover it. The way things are going, it won't be long before the only time you'll have to have your period is when you want to get pregnant."

"I mean, that's the only time you need it anyway."

"Everything is getting so much more convenient."

Listening to the two of them talk, I involuntarily pressed my hand against my belly. I had my period today. It was a hassle having it every month, but it felt kind of weird to imagine a world in which it no longer really existed. Just another thing that was disappearing from our world.

The high school where the four of us had met was in the low hills of Chiba Prefecture, and it had taken over an hour by school bus through the rice fields to get there. But now the school didn't exist. The building had been renovated and made into a center to raise children.

Anyone who didn't want to stay in Chiba and become a guinea pig in the new Experiment City had been eligible for a government subsidy to relocate. My mother had been dead-set against becoming a lab rat for the nation and left, but Mika and Emiko's parents had all stayed.

"Our hometown has completely and utterly changed now. I miss it! A bit of development would have been okay, but it's a completely new town."

"Right?"

"I know it's supposed to be an experiment with enormous implications for the world, but it's still a bit sad, isn't it?"

"Do you both sometimes go back to visit your parents?" I asked.

Mika and Emiko exchanged a glance.

"Um . . ."

"It's like they're not my parents anymore, so I kind of feel there's no point going home."

"Really? I guess so."

"I wish I could see our old friends, though. Quite a lot of them are still there."

"Your mom moved out, didn't she, Amane? Do you ever go to see her in Yokohama?"

"Yeah. She's always calling me about this or that, so I drop by sometimes."

"Aging parents are a worry, aren't they? At least from that point of view, the fact mine stayed behind means that I don't have to worry about them. Then again, it also makes it difficult for me to go see them."

My glass of champagne was now lukewarm, so I gulped it down and ordered a glass of white wine.

"I wonder if Experiment City will succeed." I said.

Mika shrugged. "Yeah, I wonder too."

"If it does succeed, all advanced countries might follow suit."

"But don't you kind of get the feeling that it'll just be a natural development? The family system isn't really appropriate for us anymore," Emiko said. "To be honest, I don't really get why people want a family. Isn't it just for convenience? But really it's more convenient not to have one, especially if you don't have children. While we're steadily evolving, it feels like the family system got stuck. It feels like we're kind of left hanging."

"I suppose so. I know what it's like to be living as three women together, and it's totally convenient. It won't be long before men can give birth too, and then I think the family system will really break down."

I chucked the bit of lime that had come with the food into my glass of wine.

"Don't do that! That's an expensive wine!"

"What's wrong? I like the taste like that."

My husband always put fruit in wine he didn't like much. I must have picked up the habit from him. Was it because we were family? As I drank the wine with the lime floating in it, I felt like I was enveloped in the smell of home and breathed a sigh of relief.

Mizuto and I often got together. It was the first time I'd ever felt so serious about a real-life lover that I wanted to meet up with him every day.

Since we lived in the same building, it was easy to meet on weekdays too. Little by little Mizuto began to get used to having sex, but he still didn't quite seem to get the point of going to all the trouble of penetration.

"It feels like you're kissing the inside of my body, which is reassuring," I explained to him.

Gradually my love for Krom was waning. Falling in love with someone new must function like a drug, helping me forget the pain of a former love. And so I'd progressively wanted something even stronger.

Mizuto was ideal for that. In addition to his apartment, there were plenty of other places in the building where we could have sex, like on the roof, where nobody ever went, or in the emergency staircase. He lived up to his name, with lots of water flowing out of him in the form of sweat, tears, and semen.

"It's weird using something I've only ever used for body eliminations to make love."

"It's like you're eliminating your emotions by making love. That's how I feel about it, anyway."

"Hmm, but the more I do it, the more I get the feeling they're amplifying inside me," Mizuto said and gave a little laugh.

"But it releases your sexual desire, doesn't it? That's how our bodies work."

"Well, I guess, but it's grueling too. It's like some kind of madness is being dragged out of my body along with the fluid. But then I want to do it again. I'll never be free of it."

"Using our genitals for making love is kind of weird."

"Right? Did everyone really make love like this in the old days?"

After sex, I'd have a shower and then lie on the bed fully dressed with Mizuto, and we'd romp around and fawn on each other like a couple of cats.

We often used to talk about our previous love affairs. Mizuto had always fallen in love with people from the other world, but it turned out I was his third real-life lover.

His favorite non-real-life lover was a purple-haired girl in an anime about the camaraderie between girls in a magicians' circus called Pink Magic Revolution, and he had lots of posters of her on the walls of his bedroom.

He also had lots of posters of the lovers he'd had before her. It was just like being inside my pouch of forty lovers that I carried around with me, and it made me happy. It felt like I was swimming in the history of all the important feelings of Mizuto and his former lovers.

"Oh, this girl's so pretty!"

"Yeah, that's a girl I was crazy about three years ago. I'm so happy you approve, Amane!"

He smiled happily, but whenever the conversation turned to his sexual desire for the women, he looked somewhat sober.

"I sometimes wonder whether this sexual desire really does exist in our bodies."

"Eh?"

"I sometimes think that the seeds for sexual desire and romantic love are planted in us by TV and manga, and only then do they grow within our body, without us realizing."

"Why do you think that?"

"Well, we're being exploited, aren't we? We're being spurred on to spend lots of money by the romantic love and sexual desire growing in our bodies. Isn't it all a plot to boost the economy?"

"No way!" I said, bursting out laughing.

Mizuto laughed too, then sat up and drank some mineral water from a bottle on the bedside table. "But there are times I really do feel like that," he said quietly. "It's like sexual desire itself disappeared long ago from human instincts and has now wormed its way back into our bodies as a parasite. I really think I'd be able to live more rationally if I didn't keep falling head over heels in love with anime characters."

"But a rational life is boring. And love is love precisely because it's irrational, isn't it? Falling in love with these girls has brought you many good things. Love is about learning to be yourself, after all. So you are the person you are now because you fell in love with them."

"Well, maybe, but . . ."

Mizuto was about to say something, but then we heard the front door open and a voice ring out: "Hello, I'm home!" We looked at each other and smiled. It was Mizuto's wife.

"Oh, Amane, you're here too?" she said. "But hey, Mizuto, you could have warned me!"

"Okay, okay," Mizuto said and went out of the room. I tidied myself up and got ready to go home. It was almost dinner time. I didn't want to interrupt their family time together.

I picked up my bag and made to leave, but Mizuto's wife hastily said, "Oh, Amane, it's lovely to see you. You're not leaving already, are you? Oh, but please do stay and have dinner with us."

"Hiya! I don't want to overstay my welcome, and anyway it's about time I went home."

"What? Don't say things like that! You're the first girlfriend he's ever brought home! I'm always telling him to get himself a real-life girlfriend, not one of those manga and anime girls. So I'm really happy he's found you. Come on, please stay and eat with us."

"Um . . ."

"Oh, but maybe your husband's waiting for you at home? In that case, why don't you bring him over too!"

"No, he's out on a date today."

"Seriously? Then that's all the more reason for you to hang out here with us."

She patted me on the back and led me to the dining room table.

"Do you like spicy food? We're having pad thai and larb gai. Oh, and green papaya salad!"

"I love it! Wow, are you cooking it yourself?"

"Yes, cooking's my hobby. Just make yourself comfortable. It won't take long."

When dinner was ready, the three of us sat around the table and toasted each other with Thai beer.

Mizuto's wife seemed genuinely pleased that he had found himself a girlfriend and chatted excitedly as she served food onto my plate.

"I hope Mizuto is being a good boyfriend to you. He can be a bit slow on the uptake, so I do worry a little."

"Oh, do give me a break," he said, looking embarrassed.

It was heartwarming to see them messing around affectionately just like brother and sister.

"There's dessert too. If you still have room, that is?"

"I'd love some, thanks."

"Just a moment, I'll go and get it ready."

As his wife went into the kitchen to prepare dessert and tea, Mizuto said to me quietly, "I'm sorry, my wife is quite overbearing. Now that I've got a girlfriend, she's been going on about wanting to see you again, so now that you're here she is super excited."

"Not at all. She's lovely."

"Eh, she's like a bossy older sister."

"Don't you want to have children, Mizuto?"

"Hmm, no, we don't really feel the need. We can enjoy life without kids, and that's what we originally decided when we got married."

"Really?"

I looked from Mizuto to his wife as she busied herself in the kitchen. Seeing the two of them getting along well as family even without children cheered me up.

"You know, seeing the two of you together makes me happy. What a lovely couple you are! I mean, you don't need to have kids to get along together as a family," I said frankly.

He looked puzzled. "But isn't it the same with you, Amane? I've greeted your husband in the elevator, and he seems like a nice man. He asks me to take good care of you, too."

"Yeah . . . but lately I've been feeling anxious. A lot of the people around me are having children without getting married. Most of them aren't married, and some even ask me why I think living with a stranger is the same as being family. How is it any different from just sharing an apartment with a friend? And I can't think of a definitive answer to that, even though Saku is really important to me."

"Oh yeah, people say similar things to me too sometimes. Like, how can you trust your savings to a complete stranger? Don't worry about it. Some people just won't ever understand."

"But I can't help feeling anxious. This idea we have of family might totally disappear in a few decades, mightn't it?" I said, almost spitting out the words.

"Of course it won't! Things'll be okay."

"Maybe . . ."

"Family's always been important to me, from when I was little, and it still is. I've always felt strongly that I wanted a family, that family is precious. It's a basic human instinct, isn't it? Not like love and work."

"I'm not sure. So, will Experiment City fail, then?"

"Nothing good can come of that place, that's for sure. There's no way that a world in which you just give birth to children without raising them in a family can function well. What's more, regardless of whether or not we have children, we humans need someone who connects us with life. I suppose that's the best way of putting it. I believe that our minds and bodies are made to want this connection. That's why people will run away from that Experiment place. We want a family, they'll say! We'll die of loneliness without one."

"I wonder . . . Yeah, maybe."

"Definitely."

"Hey, what are you talking about? Mind if I join in? Look, khanom mo kaeng! I hope the custard turned out okay."

Mizuto's wife came in carrying a tray with Thai dessert and tea.

As I ate my dessert, watching this happy couple, I felt the vague unease within me begin to subside.

"Is something wrong? Maybe it's not to your taste?" she asked with concern, noticing me sitting with my spoon stopped in midair.

"No, it's delicious. I just feel so happy, and I want to savor this wonderful dessert."

Mizuto and his wife exchanged a glance and laughed. They had similar gestures, and their faces looked somehow similar when they laughed. That was what happened over time when you lived together as family. That was the sort of creatures we were. And that was why everything would be okay.

Reciting this over and over in my mind, trying to convince myself, I pushed the sweet custard through the gap between my lips.

I took the elevator back upstairs to find my husband was already home. He was eating ochazuke.

"Oh, I'm sorry! I thought you said you were eating out today?"

"Yes, I did, but I felt a little peckish. Were you with your boyfriend, Amane?"

"Yes. Maybe I'll have some of that too," I said, helping myself to some of the rice my husband had cooked to make my own ochazuke.

Mizuto's wife's cooking was delicious, but I felt a sense of relief sitting at the dinner table eating ochazuke with my husband like this, confirmation that this was my home.

"You're so lucky having your boyfriend in the same building as you," he said happily as he ate. "You can meet him whenever you like."

"We both have work and our own home life, so it's not like we see each other every day. You want to eat meals with your family, don't you?"

My husband always heated the water for ochazuke in a saucepan. He insisted it was tastier that way, but to be honest, I couldn't tell the difference. But when I saw him enjoying the soup, saying how delicious it was, I started to feel that it really was tastier. I believed that was how a couple got to have similar tastes.

"Come to think of it, the other day I got told off for doing that thing you do—putting lime into a glass of white wine."

"You're only supposed to do that with cheap wine. It must be because you did it with something fancy, Amane."

"Oh, come off it, Saku—the other day you put orange and kiwi and other stuff in that expensive wine we were given."

"That's because it tasted cheap, even if it was expensive!"

I laughed, and felt a pain in my lower belly. My period had finished a while ago, so I was probably ovulating. Even though I was fitted with a contraceptive device so my eggs couldn't be fertilized, my ovaries still produced them. I always had a burning desire for sex when ovulating. It was like my eggs were crying out for sperm.

The infertile egg and the sperm were tangling themselves up in my belly. That was a bit creepy, I thought and absent-mindedly rubbed my sore belly.

I took some money out on my way home from work and noticed that my balance was higher than it should be. Suspicious, I put my bank book into the ATM to update it and found that, as feared, my ex-husband had deposited money in my account.

This had happened a few times before.

I didn't want to have any direct contact with him and had always returned the money through a lawyer friend of my mother's who had helped with my divorce. I would have to phone my mother to ask for the lawyer's new contact number, as I recalled hearing that she'd been transferred to a different office.

Phoning my mother was tiresome. As usual, she complained about being given things to do when her back hurt, and pestered me to come visit.

"I'll dig out her new business card, so drop by to see me."

"Yeah, okay. I'll come now," I told her with a sigh, and hung up.

It was depressing going to my mother's apartment, I thought, as I reluctantly got on the train for Yokohama.

When I arrived, she greeted me with a bag full of vegetables and fruit. "Living alone, I always have some leftover, so take them home with you."

"Thank you."

She seemed satisfied when I obediently took them.

"This is her new office in Yokohama."

"Okay."

When I split up with my ex-husband, my mother had taken his side. Remembering this, I wanted to get away quickly. "Well, Saku's waiting for me, so I'd better be going," I said.

Observing me closely, my mother smiled thinly.

"I still can't believe that sexual desire in the home is such a crime. I like your ex better than Saku, I must say. Even now your ex-husband is still desperately trying to attract your attention, and that's quite touching, isn't it?"

"What's touching about it? He tried to rape his wife! He's a pervert," I responded angrily.

My mother's smile grew wider, showing her crooked teeth. "In the old days it was men like Saku, who had women on the side, that were in the wrong, you know. What's wrong with having sex with your wife? That's how you were conceived, after all."

"Ugh, things have changed! Nowadays when you get married you swear to treat each other as family, and never think of the other sexually or romantically. Breaking that oath is an outrageous betrayal."

"I can't believe the day has come when sex between a married couple is called incest. Even brothers and sisters used to get married long ago, you know."

"I know. But the meaning of words is always changing. Common sense is completely different for us now. Just look in the dictionary. The definition of 'incest' is given as 'sexual intercourse between family members, such as between husband and wife.'"

"In the old days, falling in love with anime characters was considered perverted, you know."

"I'm fine with that. I don't care when I was born, I will fall in love with anyone I want, irrespective of whether they exist in real life or not. Love is about having the courage to be called a pervert."

She paused. "Me too, I get it. Like mother like daughter, after all. Anyway, there's no point arguing about it," she said in a low voice, no longer smiling. "As far as I'm concerned, it's all instinct. However creepy you might find it, I was simply following my instinct too, you know."

I glared at her without saying anything.

She waved her hands before her, a bitter expression on her face. "Look, you've got what you came for, so now you can leave. Go back to your nice clean house."

"I don't need to be told. I was just on my way."

My mother's apartment was packed full of old books and movies from back when it was considered natural for people to have children through copulation. The old-fashioned romance movies reflected a completely different sensibility from nowadays, and my mother was probably the only one who still watched them. They were all prewar or from the wartime period, before the major advances in artificial insemination, so the quality of the film was also mostly old and the contents monotonous.

I wasn't particularly repulsed by the people in those movies in their old-fashioned clothes falling in love, getting married, and copulating with family members. After all, that was the only way of doing things they knew back then, so it was like seeing archive material from an earlier human society, and I watched them with a clinical detachment. But when my mother tried to physically force these ideas onto me even now, I found it horrifying and nauseating. I wanted to yell at her that the world she believed was right was only one point on the spectrum between the past and present.

We humans were always changing. Whichever world we were brainwashed by, we didn't have the right to judge others based on the ideas we had been inculcated with.

I clutched hold of my bags and made to leave.

"I conceived you because I fell in love," my mother said under her breath. "But nobody understood me. By the time you were born, the world had already gone crazy. I had to remain normal all by myself."

"Mom, look. I remember reading that in primitive times men and women were wildly promiscuous. Sex was a ritual, and on the day of the ritual young people would get together and have group sex in order to conceive. But if anyone did that today they'd be considered lunatics, right? It's the same with what you're doing now. Times change. What's normal also changes. Clinging on to what was normal in the past is insanity."

"Well, you're probably right. But I was the one who brought you up. Don't you forget that. Instead of lullabies, I told you stories of the way the world is supposed to be. I'll make a prediction. You will be the last woman alive to have sex. I put a curse on you at birth so you would spend your life haunted by something that is disappearing."

"Don't be ridiculous!"

"When you were a baby, I taught you what was right so that you would be normal and not corrupted by the craziness of everyone else. I engraved it into your soul, you know. The world you first see when you're born will never vanish from your soul, however much you're infected by the present world."

I had no desire to talk about this a moment longer. I threw the bag of vegetables she'd given me onto the floor.

"What are you doing?" she shouted.

I ignored her and ran out of her apartment.

"I've cursed you with love and sex, remember it!" Her voice followed me. "The day will come when you return to your senses. However crazy society gets, you will regain your normal instinct, no doubt about it. It's engraved in your soul!"

I blocked my ears and ran out of the building. I carried on running even though I couldn't hear her voice any longer. I had the feeling that my mother's words would reach me however far I ran.

Days later my mother's words were still running around my head like a curse.

"What's up, Amane? Are you feeling unwell?"

We had come to the cafe next to the office for lunch, but I couldn't eat anything. Ami peered into my face, looking worried. "You're very pale. Don't you think you should ask your manager if you can go home early?"

"No, I'm okay. I just have a bit of an upset stomach, that's all," I said with a half-hearted smile.

Ami nodded. "Sorry if I'm presuming too much here, but I don't suppose you've already started artificial insemination, have you?"

"What?"

"It's just that I've heard that it's common to feel under the weather after removing the contraceptive device. And even more so if you've already had artificial insemination. You'd better look after yourself, you know."

"No, no," I said hastily. "I haven't started yet."

"Well, if you say so . . ." she said, still looking concerned.

"Hey, Ami. You want to have a child, don't you? Why is that? I mean, surely it's because you want a family, right?"

"What? Why these questions all of a sudden? But yeah, I mean . . ." Ami tilted her head questioningly as she ate her avocado-tuna rice bowl. "I don't really know why, I just want a family. I guess I feel that I'll be able to love a child who shares my blood. I don't really like people on the whole, but I do think that I would feel affection for my own child. So I want to meet my own child. And the only way I can do that is by giving birth to them, right? So I want to have a baby."

"Is that what you call instinct?"

"Probably. All women feel the same way to some extent, don't they?"

"You think? Yeah, maybe."

I felt reassured by the word "instinct." That was why I wanted to have a child with my husband, and to become even closer as a family. I wanted to nurture a new life in my belly. With a child, the three of us would be even further perfected as a family.

Suddenly I felt hungry and reached my fork out to the now-cold pasta in front of me.

"Amane, if you have a stomachache, you shouldn't force yourself to eat, you know."

"I've got my appetite back," I said with a smile.

"What? What are you on about? So you *have* been inseminated then! Sure sounds like it to me," Ami said with a grin.

On my next day off I had a date with Mizuto in the afternoon. There were lots of small galleries in our neighborhood, so we went to look at some paintings and then enjoyed a piece of cake in the gallery cafe.

Mizuto had been a little restless all afternoon. After we finished our cake and left the cafe, I instinctively went to hold his hand, but he slipped out of my grasp.

"It's nice weather, so how about we go to the riverbank?" he said.

The riverbank was deserted. We walked along, gazing at the light reflecting off the surface of the water.

"Mizuto, there's something you want to talk to me about, isn't there?"

"Huh?"

"If it's bad news, I want to know right away."

He hung his head despondently, just like a schoolboy being scolded by a teacher. "How did you know?"

"It's obvious."

"I can't go on like this, Amane."

"Have you fallen in love with someone else?" I asked as cheerily as I could.

He shook his head. "No, no, it's nothing like that."

"So why, then? I want to know your reasons."

I looked straight at him, and he looked up.

"I couldn't bring myself to tell you, but it's difficult," he said hoarsely. He looked so dejected I felt a rush of affection for him, and I couldn't help thinking how much I loved him in spite of myself.

"What do you mean, difficult?"

He seemed to be having trouble getting his words out, and his voice was so low I couldn't catch it.

"I'm sorry, I didn't hear what you said."

"I find sex really difficult," he muttered.

I looked at him in surprise, and he looked down, embarrassed.

"I just couldn't bring myself to say it. I do really love you, Amane, but I just can't handle sex. I tried my best because I so wanted to be with you. I thought if I could just get used to it, I'd be okay. But my feelings just got worse and worse, and I just can't anymore."

"Okay," I said in a small voice. "Okay, I get it."

Actually, I didn't get it at all. I was confused. I'd thought Mizuto and I were having sex because we loved each other. Mizuuchi's words replayed in my brain: *But isn't it just masturbation?*

Had I just been using Mizuto for masturbating, actually? And not just Mizuto. Whoever I was with, in the end, hadn't I just been using their body to pleasure myself?

Semen in which sperm couldn't swim flowed into my womb that couldn't conceive. I no longer knew what that even meant.

Maybe true sex didn't even exist anymore. Hadn't I just been masturbating, thinking I was having sex, just like Mizuuchi had pointed out to me all those years ago?

In fact, Mizuto had never put his penis into a vagina before he met me. He had never felt the need for sex in his love affairs.

I stood there rigidly, and Mizuto came close.

"I'm sorry."

But I was the one who should be apologizing. I was the one who had been using his body to pleasure myself. But the words didn't come out.

"It's okay," I said after some time. "We'll stop meeting as lovers. Can I hold your hand one last time?"

"We can do everything you want, Amane. Just for today, I want to do everything for you as your lover."

"No, it's okay. I won't touch anywhere other than your hand." I was too scared to even kiss him. Even that probably felt creepy to him.

"Let me do something. Anything is fine. Something special."

I was amused. "Well then, I want to eat your semen."

"What?"

"I want to eat your semen, Mizuto. As the last thing you do for me."

"Um . . ."

"No way, right? After all, that's why we're splitting up, obviously. Why do you say such awful things, like you'll do anything for me?" I laughed.

He took my hand. I'd only said it to lash out at him, but he led me to a place where nobody would see us.

"I can manage to get a little out. I really want to do something—anything—to make you happy, Amane."

I wasn't deranged enough to force someone to have sex with me when they didn't want to, I wanted to retort, but it felt like too much trouble to explain.

Mizuto led me to a spot under the bridge where we wouldn't be seen.

"Where shall I put it?"

I wanted to say that he didn't need to do it if he didn't want to, but the words didn't come out. I silently took an empty plastic water bottle out of my bag.

"Would you mind looking away, Amane?" he said with difficulty, his large eyes downturned.

He must have found it painful just to be seen. His orgasm was his alone, and not something I should share. I crouched down and buried my face in my arms. I would have sunk into the darkness they made before my face had it been possible.

I no longer heard Mizuto's voice. As I stared into the darkness of my arms, I'd just begun to think that maybe he had already left, when I heard him say in a small, tired voice, "It's all right now, Amane."

I looked up in relief to see him looking at me seriously, his face a little pale. He held out the bottle with a small amount of clear liquid in it.

I took it and thanked him, even though I didn't particularly want it.

I had often swallowed Mizuto's clear semen when we'd had sex together. That must have been really hard for him to bear, I now realized.

"Amane, what's it like to eat it? You said it was different from regular food, didn't you?"

"Completely different!" I almost laughed. Mizuto hadn't even understood the meaning of what I'd been doing.

"You know, I always had the feeling that you were eating a bit of me, Amane. It's true that it was hard, but it's not like everything about it was painful. It also gave me a warm feeling sometimes."

"Ah."

"Amane, thank you for eating me."

I remained crouched down, clutching the slightly warm bottle, unable to get up. "Do you think sex will disappear from the world one day?" I asked him.

"Why are you asking that all of a sudden?"

"A former lover once said that to me. It sounded like a prophecy."

"I don't really know, but I'm sure it won't. Not as long as you're around, Amane," he said gently.

I couldn't look him in the face and just kept staring at his grubby pale-blue sneakers.

"You're early, aren't you? Is everything okay?" my husband asked cheerfully when I got home.

My resolve crumbled and I burst into tears.

"Oh no," he said hastily. "What happened, Amane?"

I buried my face in his white shirt and howled. Bewildered, he stroked my back slowly.

He didn't ask me again what was wrong but just kept gently patting my back until I grew tired of crying and went to sleep.

It was already October, but my husband and I decided to play with water the way we sometimes did in summer. He'd suggested it to cheer me up since I'd been moping around.

We turned on all the heating and put a spare heater in the bathroom, and the apartment quickly warmed up.

It was as though summer had returned to our apartment while everywhere else was still cold. Amused by the ludicrous wastefulness of what we were doing, we went laughing to our individual rooms to change into our bathing suits.

I wore a shirt over my bathing suit. Even though we were family, I was not accustomed to showing any skin to my husband, and my husband felt the same way.

By the time we were ready, the bathtub was full. In long sleeves despite the heat, we headed for the bathroom, wiping sweat from our foreheads.

The bathtub was too small for us both to get in at once, so first we sat on the edge together, flutter-kicking the water with our feet. I was better at it than he was. Then we took turns getting in the tub and splashing around.

"Family is weird, isn't it? We don't show each other much skin, but then we let each other see things we wouldn't want our lovers to see, like when we throw up, for example. And we don't feel in the least embarrassed about it. Isn't that funny?"

"That's what family is. It's what makes me feel you're special, Amane. It's because we're family, of course."

"I'm looking forward to having a baby. I bet any child inheriting our genes is going to be cute. Do you want a son? Or a daughter?"

"A daughter would be nice. Oh, but girls reach puberty earlier, don't they? Before I know it, she'll be telling me she doesn't want to take baths with Papa anymore, I suppose."

"Aren't you putting the cart before the horse? Hahaha! But it's true, girls fall in love earlier, too."

Hahaha! Hahaha! Heeheehee! Hahaha! Heeheehee! We laughed, making the sounds that came from a happy home. Years later we would still be here making the same sounds of a happy family, but with the addition of our child it would all be even louder.

Family, family, family. Every time we recited this magic word, I felt reassured. Even though I'd lost a lover, I had my family. I would give birth to a baby.

I was connected to the world by my womb. And I found that reassuring.

"Hey, Saku, have you thought about names for our child?"

"Yeah, of course. Whether it's a boy or a girl, I think it should have a name that's a little old-fashioned. A bit like they could be in a historical drama."

"Mmm, that sounds good. Just right for bringing up a child with their feet firmly on the ground. A good Japanese name should have a touch of elegance to it."

"But I'd like to take a kanji character from each of our names. I mean, how about taking one of the characters in 'Amane' and somehow matching it with one of the characters from my name?"

"That's a lovely idea. I won't be able to stop thinking about that now."

We both laughed again. The sounds of our laughter overlapped and rang out around the bathroom. It was as though we were following each other's cues in a musical performance.

"Why do you want to have a child, Saku?"

"Why this question all of a sudden? I want to pass on my own genes. I'll enjoy watching a child grow up. I won't need to worry about support when I get old. The bond between you and me will deepen even further. It's more difficult to find a reason *not* to want one."

"Yes, you're right."

"Absolutely. Whatever bad things happen outside, I'll be able to forget it when I come home and hear a child laughing. Family is a lifework for everyone."

He laughed again. I also gave a dry laugh.

After splashing around for a while, my body felt heavy and tired, just as if we'd been swimming at the pool.

Feeling chilly, we wrapped ourselves in towels and ate the out-of-season watermelon that we'd left ready on the table.

"I'm thirsty. Have we got any beer?"

"Only wine. That'll make you feel even colder, you know."

"Drinking alcohol will warm us up."

He got out some red wine and brought my glass too, so I joined him, although the combination of watermelon and wine was a bit strange.

Absentmindedly, I turned on the TV just as a news report came on about the tenth round of pregnancies at the Chiba Experiment City.

The screen showed the children conceived on the tenth Christmas since the City had been founded.

Munching on his watermelon, my husband said, "The children from the first pregnancies are nine years old already. I guess by now they must know things like their multiplication tables."

"I guess so. I wonder what kind of kids they'll turn out to be."

"Me too! I'm really looking forward to knowing more about them. They're apparently super bright, having had a perfect childhood, unlike with the family system."

"I wonder. I mean, the news is so exaggerated."

"Oh, look! Isn't that right by the house you grew up in, Amane?" He leaned forward excitedly.

The TV was showing a small image of the station near where I'd grown up.

"You seem pretty interested in Experiment City," I commented. He never got this excited about anything.

"Well, not really . . ." he mumbled. "But this is incredible. Can humans really be raised outside the family system? Can you really raise children and have your offspring thrive in this other way? It's revolutionary!"

"I don't know. The experiment has only happened in small towns so far. Do you think it can really work for the whole of Chiba?" I said with a shrug. I wasn't so interested.

"It's fascinating to think about," he said, putting the watermelon he'd been eating down on the table. "Children are now born through artificial insemination, and family relationships have weakened. Oh, I don't mean you and me, Amane. I'm just saying generally."

"I know."

My husband was absorbed in watching the news, his watermelon forgotten.

"Shall we go shopping in Chiba on Sunday and see Experiment City?" he said. "The transit there is super advanced, and there are loads of big shopping malls. There is some red tape to get in, but it sounds quite easy to go for a day trip."

"Sure, but don't you have a date?"

Sunday was supposed to be his day for meeting his lover.

"Um . . . it's okay. We don't have any plans this weekend," he said in a small voice.

I suddenly noticed the bottle of wine was empty. I hadn't finished my glass yet, so he must have drunk all of it.

"We haven't got any more wine," I told him as he went to check the fridge for more.

"We've got this. Let's drink it now," he said, coming back with a bottle of Chinese baijiu someone had given him.

"Are you sure it's okay? It's forty percent alcohol, you know. Wouldn't it be better to dilute it?"

"No, it's best straight. Will you have some too, Amane?"

I shook my head.

The smell of grain alcohol came wafting over to me. My husband's cheeks and ears were bright red, probably because this was a drink he wasn't used to.

It sounded like things weren't going very well between my husband and his lover. Maybe he was drowning his sorrows. To change the subject, I gestured to the TV.

"Look at that! It used to be such a pretty park. Now there are so many apartment blocks." A park my mother had taken me to when I was little had completely changed. "It kind of looks like a model."

"It *is* a model," my husband said in a strangely forceful voice. "This is an experiment, after all. If you put people into a different system, can they continue breeding properly? Experiment City is like the box you put mice into for experiments."

"What will happen if the experiment is successful?"

"I guess the concept of family will cease to exist. I have a hunch that's what will happen." He seemed feverish. "It's far more logical. After all, even *we* don't really know what makes us family, do we? We met at a marriage party, agreed on conditions, had the feeling that we could get along, and now we live like brother and sister."

He was beginning to slur his speech. "How are people who designate themselves family any different from strangers? Nobody knows anymore. Nobody knows what makes family different from strangers anymore. In reality, we're already lost."

His breath stank of alcohol, and he was getting garrulous. He was quite drunk now, his head swaying from side to side.

I stared at his profile in silence.

Hadn't family been a precious religion for both of us until just a few moments ago? Was he showing his true feelings now that he was drunk? It was precisely because we were devout believers in the religion of family that we had felt safe living with a complete stranger.

His dark eyes were glued to the screen. "We've changed, and society is also changing to catch up with us. That's all it is."

I suddenly felt like throwing up and ran to the bathroom.

The wine I'd just drunk came welling back up, and red vomit flowed into the toilet. I thought I could hear my husband laughing in the living room.

After that evening, I took a day off work and went alone to artificial insemination counseling.

I felt that if I had a child, I could put a stop to this crazy ongoing cycle of coming into heat like an animal.

The bespectacled doctor was a kindly-looking man, a little older than me. After examining me, he explained that the procedure for artificial insemination had developed by leaps and bounds, and that it was now painless and had a high rate of success.

"Do you have any questions?" he asked.

"Um . . . can I ask something strange?"

"Of course, go ahead."

"Well . . . if artificial insemination hadn't developed this far, do you think people would still be having sex to get pregnant?"

The doctor smiled, his gentle eyes narrowing. "Well, I suppose so. If that was the only way, then that's what they would have to do."

"My parents conceived me through sex."

"Is that so? That's quite old-fashioned now, isn't it?"

"Um . . . I have another question. If men become able to get pregnant, do you think the family system will cease to exist?" I asked in a small voice.

I could still feel the sensation of the doctor's cold speculum in my vagina.

I was an animal with a womb. Sometimes when talking with my husband, I would suddenly feel that I wasn't really me, I was just his womb. There was a moment of fear when I wondered whether by chanting the word "family" over and over like a spell, my husband was putting a curse on me to make me into his womb.

"Mmm, yes, I suppose that could possibly be the case."

I didn't know how to respond to this, and my words stuck in my throat.

"This might not have anything to do with it," he said gently, "but my great uncle was buried in the ground, something that he adamantly wanted."

I couldn't say anything.

"That's old-fashioned too, isn't it? Sometimes remnants of old customs are found in unexpected places."

"Oh."

"That's all. It really is nothing special."

"Okay," I said, fighting back tears.

As far as my husband knew I was at work as usual, and it felt too awkward to go straight home after my appointment at the clinic, so I went to the park to kill time instead. I must have lost track of things, as I suddenly realized the sun was going down. I was concerned my husband might be worried, but when I opened the front door, everything was dark inside the apartment.

Maybe he went to meet his lover, I thought as I went into the living room, but my husband was there lying on the couch, his face pale.

For a moment I thought he was dead and ran over to him, but he was warm to the touch. I grabbed his shoulder, as if clinging onto that warmth.

"Saku! Saku!" I said, shaking him.

He opened his eyes sleepily. "Oh, Amane . . . you're home."

"What's the matter? Did you drink all of this?" There were several empty wine bottles lying on the table.

He stood up, holding his hand over his mouth, so I followed him to the toilet and rubbed his back as he threw up. He didn't look any better after vomiting, and he went back to the living room and lay down on the couch.

"Do you want to go to your room? I'll help you. You should get some sleep."

"No, I'm okay."

"You are not okay. Your face looks like death."

His body reacted to the word "death," and he started shaking.

At that moment, his cell phone on the table started ringing.

I looked at it and saw his lover's name on the screen.

"Saku, it's your girlfriend."

"I don't want to answer now."

"Don't be like that. Here!"

I handed him the phone and he put it to his ear, his face white.

"Hello? Um, yes . . . I'm Saku Amamiya. What? Hello?"

I could hear what sounded like a male voice faintly coming from the phone. It seemed it wasn't Saku's girlfriend after all. I stared anxiously at him.

"Yes. Yes . . . Is she safe? I see. Yes, yes . . ."

The call ended, and my husband sank down on the couch, his head in his hands.

"What's wrong? Has something happened?" I asked, rubbing his back.

"It was a paramedic," he said, as if wrenching the words out of himself. "She attempted suicide."

"What?"

"She hasn't got any family. But even if I go, seeing me will just make things worse."

"No, that's no good. Let's go right away. Which hospital is she in?"

Still holding his head in his hands, he muttered the name of a hospital in the city in a scratchy voice.

"Let's go now. Come on, get ready."

I shoved his wallet and phone into his hands, fetched my handbag, and we hurried out.

The hospital was twenty minutes away by taxi.

"I can't see her," my husband said quietly.

I left him in the corridor and went into the ward.

The room didn't have a door, making it easy for nurses to rush in at a moment's notice. The farthest bed was empty, and the one closest to the entrance had the curtain closed around it. I disinfected my hands with the alcohol provided and, since there was no door, knocked on the wall.

"Hello," I called.

The bed creaked.

"Oh, don't get up. I'm Saku's wife, Amane. Do you remember me?"

"Amane?" came a small voice. "Of course I remember you! It's sweet of you to come. I'm sorry to be in such a state."

"Not at all . . ."

"Don't stay out there. Please do come in."

The curtain swayed and a small hand appeared. I hurried over to it and went behind the curtain.

My husband's girlfriend was lying on the bed. She was a lot skinnier than she'd been a few years earlier when I'd gone out to dinner with her and my husband. She'd been thin then, but now her arms and legs were like sticks.

Her whole body looked as though it had shrunk. Her large, well-defined eyes hadn't changed, and with her short black hair they were startlingly clear against the white sheets.

Her emaciated state was a far cry from the career woman I'd met before. Now she looked more like an anorexic teenager.

"Um . . . are you feeling all right?"

Her wrists were wrapped in bandages, and she had a drip in her arm.

She gave a short laugh. "My wounds aren't that bad. The malnutrition is more serious. I got a telling-off from the doctor."

I was relieved that she sounded a bit braver than I'd feared.

"I was worried about you," I said.

"You haven't changed, Amane. It's so nice you're here. Just seeing your face is reassuring." She smiled.

I wondered whether I should tell her that my husband was in the corridor, but she looked up at me with her pitch-black eyes and said, "He's outside, isn't he?"

"Yeah . . ."

My husband was probably sitting nervously on a chair outside. Now and then I could hear the rubber soles of his shoes squeaking against the floor. Our conversation was probably leaking out into the corridor.

"Well then, tell him that I won't see him ever again."

I gulped, but her gaze never wavered.

"Don't you love Saku anymore?" I asked her.

"I love him. That's why I can't see him."

Were these words echoing around the corridor too? I had the sensation of a cold draft floating in from outside.

"Um, right now you're upset, so let's talk about it when you're feeling calmer—"

"No. Tell him now. My mind's made up."

"Saku is still in love with you, you know," I managed to squeeze out, unable to avert my eyes from hers.

"And I with him. But it's never going to work." She gave a little sigh and looked up at the ceiling. "We humans are no longer capable of being in love."

She touched her chest with a skinny finger, as though stroking her own heart.

"Saku is important to me, but I no longer understand the emotion that we call love. But Saku is obsessed with it, sometimes so much that I get scared of him. It's like he turns me into a mechanical doll that falls in love."

"Um . . . why don't the two of you talk it over? I'm sure you'll find a way to work things out—"

"No, it's not going to work. I'm sorry that I couldn't love your husband well enough."

She gave a little smile. She had been sitting motionless but now rotated her body and stretched out her arm with the drip attached toward me.

Her glossy black hair seemed to swim in the sheets as she stretched her thin fingers out to me. I realized she was asking me to shake hands.

Bewildered, I squeezed her small hand.

"Tell him I said goodbye."

There was no warmth either in her voice or in her hand.

I nodded slightly, thinking that it was as if she were already dead.

My husband was sitting in the chair in the corridor outside the room.

"Did you hear?" I asked in a small voice, and my husband smiled weakly and gave a faint nod.

We headed home in silence.

Before I realized it, we were holding hands. My husband's hand was cold, just like his lover's had been.

"It's snowing. Even though it's only October," he murmured.

I wondered if he was seeing things, but when I looked up, there were indeed shiny white flakes coming down out of the black sky.

When I looked more closely, I realized it wasn't snow but raindrops, shimmering like snow as they reflected the streetlights.

I was captivated by the countless shining drops coming down, but the fine drizzle was gradually getting stronger and turning into big black lumps that were beginning to make us wet.

"Oh, it's already turned to rain. It didn't last long."

Maybe snow really had been falling on my husband. Shiny drops still glittered in his hair.

I gave his freezing cold hand a strong squeeze. His bones wriggled in my grasp.

"Should we elope?" he suddenly said.

"What?"

"You and I are still obsessed with pretending to fall in love and have sex, even though those things are already disappearing from the world . . . I can't take it anymore." His bones trembled in my hand. "Let's run away together to a world where romantic love doesn't exist," he said hoarsely.

What a strange thing to say, I thought. Eloping didn't exist anymore. Wasn't it something that two people used to do in the long distant past when they fell in love? Still, I agreed without hesitation.

"Yeah, okay. Let's run away."

My husband was my family. He was the one whose existence I had to protect. If he said we should run away, I would do it. I would bring along his spirit to wherever he wanted to go, I thought.

"It's already nearly the end of October. We don't have much time."

We might be eloping, but we still needed to apply for an entry permit to Experiment City in Chiba. We went straight to the ward office to take care of the formalities.

Our departure date was set for two weeks after the night the shining flakes had fallen. At that point in time, our marital relationship would be dissolved on paper, although we wouldn't be removing our wedding rings.

We also signed a pledge agreeing to stay in Chiba for a minimum of two years.

We left our jobs and would be seeking new employment in Chiba. We weren't telling anyone we were going to Chiba, and my boss and colleagues probably thought I was pregnant, because they wished me good luck.

As we started making all the arrangements, it occurred to me that there was now nothing in my life other than my husband and our future child. This was an extremely happy discovery.

"I'm sorry to bring you along in all this, Amane," my husband said in a small voice as we were packing.

"What are you talking about? We're family, aren't we? If you're going to elope, you do it as a family, right?"

I smiled at him, and finally his expression softened.

On the day of the move, we got a moving company to take care of the big items and put a few personal belongings into a bag to take with us on the train to Chiba.

As we entered Chiba, the confused urban sprawl outside the train window gradually gave way to a world of white buildings and greenery.

The carriage had bench seats along each side, and we sat next to each other gazing through the window opposite us, as though watching a movie.

To enter Chiba, we would first have to go through the border procedures at Narita. It was just as if we were traveling abroad.

Now and then the train entered a small tunnel, and each time the view outside the window went black, and we were left with only the faint lights in the carriage. I squeezed my husband's hand harder.

"Hey, don't you think we're a bit like Hansel and Gretel?"

"You mean running away holding hands? Isn't it more like Tyltyl and Mytyl?"

"You're right. We're going in search of the Blue Bird, you and I."

There was nothing funny about this at all, but we looked at each other and laughed.

It was like we were running away from something, but also like we were chasing after something. Either way, we were family and we shared the same fate.

"We're going to stay together as a family even though we'll be in Chiba, aren't we?"

"Of course we are! We'll never give up our child to the Center! We'll bring it up in secret, just the two of us."

As the train came out of the tunnel, light flooded in through the windows and filled the carriage where we were sitting holding hands.

Our neatly aligned toes cast small shadows in the light.

PART THREE

Awoken from my doze by a far-off train announcement, I opened my eyes a crack.

It was evening outside. People were picking up their luggage and getting off the train.

I could hear the sound of a plane in the distance. It sounded like the distant roar of a huge animal.

My husband was sleeping next to me, and I shook him awake.

"Saku, we're here."

"Ah . . ." he said and opened his eyes sleepily.

We hurriedly picked up our bags, got off the train, and headed for Narita Airport.

To enter Chiba, we had to go through immigration at Narita. Casting sidelong glances at a line of people with large suitcases, we headed to the almost-deserted prefectural immigration desk. Just like when going abroad, we were grilled about whether we were traveling as tourists or immigrating, and if the latter, whether we had the necessary permits, whether we were the applicants or representatives of the applicants, and so forth. By the time we got through the gate, it was beginning to get dark outside.

We got on the direct bus to Experiment City from Narita Airport, and after an hour of being shaken around we arrived at the town where we were going to live. It was completely dark by then. We wandered along in the faint light from the streetlamps and the glow that seeped out from apartment windows, finally arriving at the apartment block where we were going to live.

The formalities had already been completed in advance, and the landlord, who lived on the eighth floor, gave us our keys.

My husband's apartment was number 705, and mine was next door in 704. Both were studio apartments, and we decided to make my husband's our bedroom, and mine would be the living room.

Exhausted, we sat in my empty apartment eating the bentos we'd bought at Narita Airport without heating them up, then went to 705, got into the sleeping bags we'd brought with us, and slept on the floor.

"It's a bit like camping, isn't it?"

"The beds will arrive tomorrow. Then we'll really be able to start our new life."

We chatted quietly, our bodies tired but our eyes wide open. We had always slept in separate rooms, and I hadn't known that my husband couldn't sleep unless the room was completely dark. We didn't have curtains yet, so the light from all the other apartments came in.

As we chatted about nothing in particular, like how the lights in the small windows in the tower block opposite ours were like stars, my husband sneezed.

"Are you cold? The heating's on, but . . . do you want to come closer?"

"Thanks."

Our shoulders touching, we closed our eyes. That moment was probably the closest we'd physically been to each other in our entire marriage.

As always, my husband's body heat was a simple warmth without any hint of sexuality, like that of a cat or a little bird. Relieved, I sank into that warmth as I fell asleep.

I woke up to sunlight streaming through the window.

I got up and looked out the window, and I got a shock. It had been dark when we arrived, so I hadn't realized, but looking outside I saw that the city was extremely well-organized and surprisingly beautiful.

When I gazed out over the city from above like this, it looked like a model. Pure-white apartment blocks stretched out into the distance, and a pale-blue promenade ran through the center. The streets were lined with yellowish-green trees as far as the eye could see.

There were numerous parks, all filled with pale-blue gravel. The square outside the station was covered in pale-blue concrete. I could see a few small figures walking over it. It felt like we were living in the sky.

Taking care not to wake my husband, I left the apartment and headed to a nearby convenience store.

It must have been ten years since this city was built, but looking around, I was amazed that a ten-year-old city could be this clean.

I did my shopping and returned to the apartment to find my husband awake and folding up the sleeping bags.

"Oh, there you are. Where did you go? I was just about to go look for you in the living room."

"I went to get breakfast. Here," I said, passing him some mineral water and a sandwich, and he took them, looking pleased.

"Thank you."

The moving company was due to arrive with our belongings today. It took time to complete all the formalities to move to Chiba, and the truck had to pass through controls at Narita, so the delivery had been scheduled for the day after we arrived.

We finished our meal and were just cleaning the apartment when the doorbell rang.

"The beds go in this apartment. Oh, the refrigerator goes next door. The table too."

The delivery men looked perplexed as we separated the furniture between the two apartments, but they finished the job, and we thanked them as they left.

There might be two outside doors, but this was our home. We arranged our shared living space between the two identical apartments, the sofa and table in my apartment, the beds and dressing room in my husband's.

When we'd more or less finished sorting everything out, we went upstairs to greet our landlord. It had been late when we'd gone to collect our keys last night, and we hadn't been able to speak much.

"It's unusual to have two friends living next door to each other."

The landlord was a kindly-looking middle-aged man. He looked at us and smiled.

In this city, everyone was expected to live alone. The concepts of couples and family were considered disruptive for public morals and unsuitable for Experiment City.

"Yes, we're close friends," I replied carefully, avoiding saying anything to give away the fact we were a couple. "We both like cooking and always make far too much, so it's handy to live close by so we can share."

"Really? That's great! I always have ready-made meals."

"Oh, in that case we'll bring some food for you too," my husband said.

"I'd love that," he said, the corners of his eyes crinkling as he smiled. He didn't look at all suspicious of our friendship.

"Have you been to the park? Today's a weekday, but you'll be able to play with the Kodomo-chans this afternoon."

"No, not yet," my husband said, shaking his head.

"Shall I take you there? We could meet in front of the apartments at three o'clock."

"Yes, please!" my husband answered enthusiastically.

I was tired and would have preferred to rest, but I forced a smile and said, "I'd like to go too."

"Well then, see you later. This is a lovely place to live. Please do let me know if you have any problems," he said with a friendly smile.

"Thank you so much," we replied, and bowed.

The landlord took us to the large park by the station. It was covered in pale-blue gravel, it felt like walking in the sky.

As we entered the park, the Kodomo-chans all turned in unison to look at us.

"Mother!"

"Hello, Mother!"

All the children were dressed in white smocks and had their hair cut in identical bobs reaching just below their ears. At first glance it was impossible to tell which were boys and which were girls.

"Yes, yes, come to Mother," the landlord said with a smile to one Kodomo-chan who came running excitedly over to us, and hugged it.

I'd known from news reports that everyone here was Mother to all the children, who were all called Kodomo-chans, but I was still taken aback to actually experience this.

Experiment City had only started ten years ago, so there were just adults and children up to the age of nine. All the children were divided into groups according to age, with babies in a specialist building, and preschool children playing under the supervision of the Center staff. The older children were unsupervised, playing soccer or on swings.

I was bewildered to have children I had never met before clinging to me and calling me Mother, and I had no idea what to do with them. My husband was delightedly stroking the heads of the Kodomo-chans who came up to him.

The Kodomo-chans were used to behaving like pet animals.

The landlord picked up one of the Kodomo-chans flocking together like pigeons and said, "That's right, please treat them affectionately. Our important role as Mothers is to ensure they constantly feel loved as children of all humankind."

Still feeling disoriented, I tried stroking the head of the Kodomo-chan who was clinging onto the hem of my skirt. It was extremely warm, and its entire body was squishy and soft. It gave me the creeps.

There were a lot of other Mothers in the park besides us, including young women and middle-aged men. Dressed in white smocks and shorts, the Kodomo-chans were being gently stroked by numerous Mothers, spoken to sweetly, and showered with love and affection. Seen from a distance, they looked like angels frolicking in the sky.

A staff member came over to talk to us. "Is this your first time participating in Mother activities?"

"Yes, we just moved here last night."

"Don't be nervous, and just enjoy playing with the children, okay? Please show them affection however you like. Whatever affection you shower on them, they will absorb it all."

The staff member was dressed in a white suit and had his hair cut in a short bob just like the children. I'd heard on the news that the staff were not Mothers, but rather like elder siblings who were on hand for the Kodomo-chans at all times. And it was true, the Kodomo-chans were not spoiled by the staff, and it was only we Mothers they clung to.

My husband was completely absorbed in stroking the Kodomo-chans' heads and hugging them. I timidly tried picking up a small Kodomo-chan who was clinging to my leg.

Its body was soft like white asparagus and felt like it might snap or break if I was careless. Seeing me looking flustered, the staff member said, "Support their bottom and back when you hold them, like this," and demonstrated with practiced movements the correct way to hold them.

When the Kodomo-chan was finally settled in my arms, it seemed to feel genuinely safe and rubbed itself against my face, smiling.

There was also a Kodomo-chan crying in a sandpit a short distance away. Adults were comforting it in different ways, laughing, as though they were actually having fun.

"Ahh, this one seems to be wetting its pants!"

"Oh dear! Let me deal with it . . ."

Kodomo-chans still in diapers were particularly popular, and everyone gleefully took care of changing them. Those crying and wetting themselves were considered special joys.

Adults flocked around the children as if they were feeding stray cats in the park, petting them and exclaiming how cute they were.

It was as though the whole town were keeping human children as pets. The staff members were on hand at all times while the Mothers cuddled the Kodomo-chans, waiting at the ready in case they were needed.

"Come here, Kodomo-chan, come over here!" my husband called, leaning down to pick up one with its identical short bobbed hair and white smock.

The Kodomo-chan in my husband's arms seemed to be used to people, and obediently let him stroke its cheek. A member of the staff came over and said, "This one likes being rubbed on the back." When my husband rubbed its back, the child wriggled in delight as though being tickled and gave a high, shrill laugh.

"Can I give it some of those cookies?" my husband asked, wiping the child's nose.

"Yes, you can give them up to one hundred kilocalories. Those are specially made cookies, so please only give them those."

We each took one of the small special cookies, broke them into pieces, and gave them to the Kodomo-chans, who ate them happily. Some warm saliva from one of them stuck to my fingertips, and I grimaced.

My husband looked so happy, exclaiming how cute they were, but I felt a chill. Everyone was doting on the children as though they were pets, and then going home alone and free without taking any responsibility for them. To be honest, I doubted whether this was enough to make the children feel they were loved by society.

"It's a bit like a cat cafe, isn't it? Petting them without being responsible for them, and when you've had enough you can just go home," I said sarcastically, but my husband just laughed and agreed.

"Ha ha, yes, it is! It's like a large-scale baby cafe. Hey, look at that one running around over there!"

I thought the entire scene was weird, my happy-looking husband included. And the Kodomo-chans, in their white smocks with identical haircuts, created an eerie atmosphere.

"So what do you think?" the landlord asked us, coming over with a child in his arms. "The Kodomo-chans are so sweet, aren't they?"

I suddenly realized what was making me feel so uncomfortable. The Kodomo-chans all had different genetic backgrounds, so their facial features were different. But the child my husband was holding and the child the landlord was holding both had exactly the same facial expressions.

The Kodomo-chan with a big nose in my husband's arms and the dark-skinned Kodomo-chan gazing up at the landlord's face were both using precisely the same facial muscle movements to narrow their eyes and open their mouths as they made a smile. I looked around more closely and saw that even the staff members, who were like the Kodomo-chans' elder brothers and sisters, were smiling in precisely the same way.

Children learned by watching adults. The staff members who looked after them all had the same hairstyle, the same facial expressions, and the same way of talking, so it was only natural that the Kodomo-chans had this imprinted on them and as they grew up would also come to have the same facial expressions.

I was flabbergasted. Was this place a kind of factory to manufacture uniformly convenient people?

My husband was oblivious as he hugged the Kodomo-chan. Another Kodomo-chan was clinging to my legs and opening its eyes and raising the corners of its mouth in a smile in precisely the same way the one in my husband's arms had.

I involuntarily pulled my leg away, and the Kodomo-chan started wailing. Its facial muscles twisted in exactly the same way as several other Kodomo-chans who were crying a short distance away.

"Oh dear, oh dear, what's the matter?" asked another Mother as she came over and happily picked up the crying child.

"Come on, Amane, that's no good. You have to shower the children with affection!"

My husband's laughing voice sounded dissonant, as though the world was creaking.

In Experiment City: Paradise-Eden, children are being raised in a new system. The Paradise-Eden system has been perfected by thorough research from the disciplines of psychology and sociology. Numerous research centers have published papers showing that the family system is an unsuitable method of reproduction for highly intelligent animals. In Paradise-Eden everyone is the child of all humankind, and everyone the mother of all humankind. This recalls the love-filled world that existed before Adam and Eve ate the forbidden fruit.

The Center provides humankind's offspring with the feed and nests necessary for their upbringing. All children at the Center are educated with a bespoke curriculum adapted to their individual brain development and psychological makeup. By controlling their lifestyle, each child can be raised to be an outstanding, capable human resource.

Adults in Paradise-Eden have two obligations. The first is to physically undergo insemination and breeding, regardless of age or sex, upon receipt of the postcard notifying selection. The second is to help nurture all children on a mental level. Specifically, all adults must be present to shower the children with affection.

Recent research has shown that children raised to feel loved by the whole world are more intelligent and more emotionally stable than those brought up under the former family system. Please be present to shower affection on children and thus continue the life of humankind. Please make sure to love all of the children as their Mother. Please make sure to shower affection continually! Thank you for coming to today's seminar. We hope you will have a wonderful life in Paradise-Eden.

We also hold weekly seminars in Paradise-Eden for residents. Please attend them if there is anything you are unsure of, or you wish to learn more about the system.

I awoke with a start in a pitch-black room.

Hearing the snoring next to me, I remembered that this was the bedroom I shared with my husband. I quietly sat up and took the Prada pouch from my bedside table. Opening it,

I rummaged around, looking by the light of the moon at the numerous lovers I kept there until I felt a little calmer.

Since we'd moved to this town, I often dreamed of the seminar I'd attended before we came here. At the time, I was dead set on the idea of going somewhere far away with my husband and hardly listened to what we were told. But now that I actually had to play with the children every day, I vividly recalled the video I'd been shown and the explanations of the staff.

This world was insane. Here, the two of us had to work to retain our normality! Gazing at my forty lovers, I could confirm the existence of my sexual urges, frozen within me. Even if there was no such thing as romantic love here, my love for all these nonreal people had accumulated in my body over the years and still existed safely within me. Even if I couldn't find a new lover in this world of Mothers, I could take the love frozen within me out of my body and gaze upon it and feel at peace in my new life.

I softly kissed the Krom key chain that dangled from my pouch. Krom was just as vivid here as he was in the other world as he gazed unflinchingly back at me.

I continued to feel a bit out of place, but otherwise things were going well.

The town was clean and new, and subsidies meant that our rent was cheap.

The town basically provided everything we needed. I took a job referred by the state and became an office worker in a small company in a part of Experiment City that was fifteen minutes away by train. My husband got a job in city hall, by the station.

We spent our weekends together in the neighborhood park with the Kodomo-chans, since it was our duty as residents to shower the children with affection. During the week, my husband and I would go to our own apartments after work, then contact each other to have dinner together.

I often had overtime at work, and my husband often returned from his job in city hall before me. Both of us earned about two-thirds of what we used to, but we weren't particularly dissatisfied with this. If I had any complaint, it was that whenever we wanted to go outside Chiba, before getting the train we first had to go to Narita and fill out lots of forms, which was too much of a bother. In Chiba we had big shopping malls and plenty of entertainment facilities, so we gradually ended up doing everything here.

"This is a happy life, isn't it?" my husband said over dinner in the living room. "The Kodomo-chans are so cute, and when I come home I have you, Amane. Did you see that child on the swing today? When I gave it some cookies, it politely bowed its head and thanked me. So cute! And all these children are mine—it's like a dream come true!"

"What are you talking about? Our child hasn't been born yet, has it?" I blurted out sharply.

"Oh . . . um, I guess. Right," he said in a tired voice.

"There's something so weird about the Paradise-Eden system, though. I think it's failing."

"Yes, there is," he agreed, but still carried on talking eagerly about how cute the Kodomo-chan he'd met today had been.

"The notices for artificial insemination will be sent out soon, won't they?"

"Yes, that's right. I hope one of us will get one, Amane."

We looked at each other and smiled.

The population levels were managed by computer algorithms, and those selected for artificial insemination would be notified by postcard in mid-November. The chosen people would be inseminated all at once, on December 24.

The postcards arrived a few days later. Nervously we opened our cards. Both of us had made the selection! We whooped for joy, and that night we celebrated.

I had my contraceptive device removed and took some medicine to stimulate ovulation, and my husband provided his sperm to the hospital, and then we excitedly waited for December 24.

We could hardly wait for the day to come, marking the time off on the calendar.

When it finally came, Christmas Eve was a beautiful, clear day without a cloud in the sky.

The hospitals were already extremely crowded by the time we arrived. My husband and I had taken the day off work and headed that morning for our local maternity and gynecology department.

When I arrived at the hospital, a doctor in a white coat with a troubled look on his face surreptitiously beckoned me over. It was Mizuuchi, my first real-life lover, who was now going to help me and my husband enact our plan.

"I'm sorry to put you to so much trouble, Mizuuchi."

"You haven't been seen by anyone, have you?" he asked me.

"No, don't worry."

He cautiously closed the door and handed me and my husband cards with numbers on them.

"Here you are. These numbers will ensure that you will be inseminated with your husband's sperm, and your husband will receive your eggs inseminated with his own sperm."

"Thank you so much. I owe you so much."

"Don't worry about that. Just make sure that you don't say anything about this to anyone. If I'm ever found out, I'll be expelled from Chiba."

"I'm really sorry for causing you so much trouble," I said and bowed my head.

Mizuuchi had realized the dream he'd told me about long ago when we were at school together, and was now a doctor researching artificial insemination and pregnancy for men. When I'd heard about his job, I had pestered him to do this for us until he eventually agreed.

"I am still just an assistant, so I can't do the artificial insemination directly myself. This is as much as I can do, okay?"

"Yes, it's enough. Thank you so much. Really, I'm so grateful."

"Well, that's okay, as long as I don't get found out. But still, I wonder why this is so important to you," Mizuuchi said with a shrug, apparently unable to understand our need to make "our" baby with my eggs and my husband's sperm.

"One of our former classmates who stayed in Chiba happens to be here too," he said. "She used to be friends with you, she's called, um . . ."

"Yumi?"

"That's right. I happened to be in charge of her preliminary examination."

"I know."

I'd heard about Yumi from a classmate. When Chiba had been turned into Experiment City ten years ago, she had stayed and had twice become pregnant and given birth to children now being raised by the Center. I just couldn't understand how anyone could blithely turn over a baby for whom they had endured the pain of childbirth only for that baby to become a Kodomo-chan.

"It's the first time anyone has gone to such lengths to be inseminated with a particular person's sperm, though . . ."

He looked so perplexed that I smiled amiably and spelled it out for him.

"We want to leave our own genes. We don't want a Kodomo-chan, we want our own child."

"I just don't understand it."

"You don't need to."

Mizuuchi had already been brainwashed by this town, I thought, smiling a little disdainfully. He looked at me with exactly the same expression on his face. "You're still not free of the brainwashing of the other world, are you?" he said.

I could feel my hole being opened wide with a cold tool.

I had never got used to this sensation, however many times I'd experienced it. A curtain had been drawn across the pelvic examination table so I couldn't see what was going on and could only hear the sound of the speculum and feel the cold metal inside my vagina. I didn't even know what shape the instrument was, and I couldn't imagine what my own vagina looked like now. It didn't hurt, but I always felt a bit scared, and my hands were so tightly clenched that my veins were popping.

"The ovulation drug has done its job. You are just about to start ovulating. The perfect condition for being inseminated," I heard the doctor say on the other side of the curtain.

I felt a different tool go into my vagina. "This will feel a little cold," I heard him say, then felt water being flushed into my vagina and flowing out again.

"And now I shall proceed to the insemination. It will only take a moment, so please relax."

It felt like a soft tube was being inserted inside me, but thinking about it made me frightened, so I stared at the ceiling, doing my best not to imagine what was happening.

The sperm my husband had delivered in advance had been frozen and was now entering me. Hugely grateful to Mizuuchi for arranging this despite the trouble it caused him, I recalled the disdainful smile he'd given me earlier.

He'd used the words "the other world," but he no longer meant the world Lapis lived in. He probably didn't even remember Lapis now. Mizuuchi was a Mother now.

People were now the only animals to reproduce by scientific means. If artificial insemination hadn't developed to this extent, we would still be copulating the way my mother had done. If there were a parallel world in which artificial insemination hadn't developed this far, what kind of animal would we be?

"All done," came the doctor's voice.

The insemination was over. It hadn't hurt at all, and I didn't even know what had actually been done to me.

"Thank you. It didn't hurt at all."

"Feeling pain is something you'll only hear about during times of war now. Technology has developed a lot. It is almost a hundred percent sure that the insemination has been successful. You will give birth next year around the end of August or September. Please look after yourself well until then."

I thanked the doctor and got off the examination table. As I put on my underpants and skirt, I wondered vaguely whether this was now the closest humans came to copulation.

I stroked my lower belly, but I didn't feel in the slightest uncomfortable. I couldn't actually feel that my husband's sperm had been quietly inserted into me.

Beyond the curtain I heard the nurse preparing the tools for the next insemination. I wondered whether there had been the sound of clean tools being laid out when I was born.

Back when people had still been animals, what sort of sounds had there been during copulation and birth? However hard I tried to imagine it, all I could bring to mind was the sight of a clean hospital.

My husband's operation was completed in the afternoon.

I'd heard that to attach the artificial womb, they would make an incision in his belly and insert tubes to circulate blood and moisture, then attach a sac made from artificial skin just above the belly button. I'd thought it would be a major operation, but it apparently only took an hour, and I was drinking coffee in a Starbucks inside the hospital when my husband finally came in waving a hand in the air.

"You got through it! How was it?"

"The operation itself was simple, but the place was packed. Lots of menopausal women or other women who can't get pregnant with their own womb for some reason or other, and of course lots of men too, so I had to wait for ages."

"I wonder why they have to do all of it on this one day?"

"Who knows? It does make me think of a virgin birth, though. Maybe it's a suitable day for that?"

My husband was wearing an extremely long sweater that came down to just above his knees. The technology hadn't yet been developed for a flexible womb that would expand as the baby grew, and people fitted with the current model of artificial womb had to live with a sac of artificial skin hanging from just above their belly button down to almost their knees. The baby would grow in this sac. To keep it hidden, therefore, they had to wear long baggy clothes, and my husband had proudly put on his male pregnancy sweater that morning.

The taxis were all busy, so the landlord had kindly offered to pick us up by car. As soon as the operation was over, we called him, and he came to the hospital straightaway.

"Thank you so much, we really appreciate it."

"Not at all. It's our duty as Mothers to help other Mothers when they've been inseminated, you know. Don't worry about it. Please, do get in."

We got into the back seat of the landlord's car together, my husband sliding in shielding his belly protectively.

"Whereabouts is the egg?" I asked him.

"It's apparently still above the belly button. They told me it would gradually move down as it grows."

"So most of the sac is empty then?"

"Yes, but the baby will gradually move down, filling it as it grows, according to the doctor."

My husband was happily leafing through a pamphlet that had headings like "How to Have a Safe Pregnancy" and "What Men Need to Be Careful of When Pregnant."

"Doesn't that sac get in the way when you move?"

"A little. But it actually feels kind of nice. It gives the feeling of raising a new life, doesn't it? It's a bit like being reborn with a new body."

I got my husband to roll up his long sweater to show me the sac. Hanging there was an odd thing that looked like a huge flattened testicle. Unlike a woman's womb, it was outside the body, so whether it could withstand external shocks was a concern. No wonder there hadn't yet been any examples of it being a success, I thought to myself, but my husband was happily stroking it, so I kept my mouth shut.

"So is it the first time for the two of you to be artificially inseminated?" the landlord asked my husband. "Did you get inseminated or go through pregnancy in the world out there?"

"No, we didn't."

"Well, good job. You must feel tired with it being your first time."

"Oh, but the reason we moved here was because we wanted to try it," my husband answered enthusiastically.

The landlord nodded and smiled. "I understand. Men can only experience pregnancy if they live in this town. But you're lucky. Not everyone gets to be inseminated straight after moving here. I also used to live in the other world, and I had kids there too, but I really wanted to experience pregnancy myself, so when Experiment City was started ten years ago, I moved here right away. But my notification didn't come for ages. Finally, after three years I got inseminated for the first time, and I've done it three more times since then."

"Really? So you're an old hand at this, then," my husband said happily.

"Yes," the landlord nodded. "I did feel a bit weird about the womb at first. But then I felt it gradually becoming part of my own body, and I was happy. You definitely can't get that experience in the other world, can you?"

"Not at all. It's still years away from being broadly viable."

"Both in terms of the technology and the cost. Hopefully there will be a successful case soon. Do your best! If there's anything you need, just tell me. I'm hoping you'll give birth to a healthy Kodomo-chan."

"I will!" my husband answered enthusiastically, nodding happily at him.

When we got home, we skipped the housework and got some pizza, then sat together on the sofa, rubbing each other's bellies.

"Your belly hasn't changed in the slightest, has it, Amane?"

"Of course not! I've only just been inseminated."

"Women are lucky. But my sac is quite something. I wonder which will be born first. I hope we don't get found out for not sending our babies to the Center."

"We're definitely going to keep them. They are ours, after all."

"I hope they're both born safely."

"If so, we'll bring them up to be siblings that get along well together."

I could see the pale-blue concrete of the station plaza through the window. A white Christmas tree with pale-blue lights had been placed in the center.

This time next year I would be gazing up at the holiday lights together with our child.

It would still be too small to understand, but we would put presents by its pillow, I thought, stroking my belly. Even though Christmas this year wasn't over yet, I could already see next year's lights flickering behind my eyelids.

The following month I miscarried.

I was at work when suddenly I started bleeding. I applied a sanitary pad and hurried to the hospital. I had been taking care of my body carefully and avoiding strenuous exercise.

"Miscarriages at this time are very common," the doctor told me calmly. "The computers take this all into account, so please don't worry about it. Get well soon."

The doctor seemed to be telling me it was all in the calculations so there was no need to worry. I wanted to shout at him that it was my child that I'd lost, not one I was carrying for humankind, but I couldn't even do that.

My treatment was over quickly. I was more upset by the doctor and nurses telling me that everything was okay because someone else's birth would make up for it than I was at having lost my baby.

"That's all for now. Well then, good luck with your next insemination," the nurse told me with a bright smile as I was leaving the treatment room, and I desperately repressed the urge to lunge at her.

Maybe nobody was even able to imagine this kind of pain anymore.

Without a word I took a taxi home, and my husband came out to meet me.

"Are you okay, Amane?"

"Yeah, I'm okay, but . . . the baby . . ."

"Well, I'm glad that you are safe, at least," he said gently, rubbing my shoulder, and the tears welled up in me.

At last I was with someone with whom I could have a normal conversation.

I buried my face in my husband's shoulder. After a while, realizing I had to try to put on a brave face, I looked up and said as brightly as I could manage, "Yes, you're right. And what's more, your baby is still okay, Saku."

"Yes, it is. I'll give birth instead of you."

My husband hugged me and stroked my back the way he did with the Kodomo-chans.

I felt the wrinkled sac hanging from his belly against my thigh as he hugged me. Did an organ resembling that exist within my belly? I wanted to take my own womb out of my belly so I could see it. And I wanted to smell the blood of the child that had been inside it.

Safely nestled against my husband's chest, I stroked his warm womb. Both my husband and his womb were warm. I closed my eyes, secure in the warmth of family.

Snow had started falling outside, and it was as though it absorbed all sound.

My husband's abdomen was growing steadily bigger. The wrinkled womb was gradually filling up as the baby grew within it.

The artificial skin was said to be specially designed to protect the inside from external shocks, but you could clearly make out the shape of the fetus through the skin, so I was a bit uneasy. It looked as though it could be easily crushed or otherwise injured, so I was extremely careful when I was around my husband.

"You don't need to be so nervous, you know. Look, try pressing my womb with your finger. See? The force is absorbed like a sponge. The baby is well protected, you know."

"But it's like it's wrapped in flesh-colored plastic wrap, and you can even see the shape of the child. I'm scared of crushing it."

"I understand, but there's no need to be worried. Look, try stroking it."

I was too scared to touch the baby, but my husband was eagerly stroking his own belly and enjoying talking to it.

Everyone wanted to talk to my pregnant husband when we were out.

"The baby seems to be doing well even though you're a man, doesn't it? Please, take my seat!"

"Thank you."

People giving up their seat for him on the train and wanting to touch his belly in the park were everyday occurrences.

"We're all hoping you give birth to a healthy Kodomo-chan!"

The way the Mothers, all full of smiles, stroked my husband's womb seemed to assert that the baby belonged to all of humankind, not to my husband. My husband also responded gleefully to the physical contact with the Mothers.

This made me feel suddenly anxious.

"Hey, we are family, aren't we?" I asked him to be sure.

"What? Oh, um, yes, of course we are!" my husband nodded.

He no longer ate much of the food I made. For my part, I couldn't help feeling that food he had cut and peeled with his hands was somehow dirty. We still sat at the same dinner table, but we each ate only the food that we had prepared ourselves.

My home will be cleaner without a complete stranger living there, I recalled Ami once saying.

We were beginning to get used to living alone in our clean homes as separate life forms not belonging to anything.

Daily life and sexual desire were matters to be dealt with alone. I was even beginning to feel that I was more suited to that kind of lifestyle.

I was relieved whenever my husband called saying he'd be late getting home. When that went on for over a week, I almost began to think that being alone was the right way to live.

We started often spending weekends alone too.

"What are you doing today?" I asked my husband by phone one Saturday morning.

"Well," he said hesitantly, "there's a movie I want to see today, so . . . and after that I'm thinking of going to the Baby Room at the Center."

"I see. I'm planning to do the laundry today, so shall we spend the day apart?"

"What about this evening? Do you want to eat together, Amane?"

"Um . . . well, I've been given some ready-made dishes, but I don't think they're really to your taste, Saku. They need eating soon, though, so I was thinking of having dinner alone today."

"Okay. I guess we'll go our own ways today, then. I'll call you again next week."

My apartment was supposed to be our shared living room, but we now had a sofa bed in there and a small table in our shared bedroom in my husband's apartment and had come to eat and sleep separately in our own apartments.

Relieved, I hung up and relaxed back onto the sofa. It was nice having my own room all to myself.

The smell of a two-person home that had previously permeated my apartment was diminishing, and I was beginning to feel comfortable living in my own smell alone.

It probably felt much like this inside the artificial womb where our baby slept, it occurred to me.

By the time spring arrived, my husband and I were contacting each other only now and again.

Juri came to visit me at the beginning of March.

"What about Saku? He's off work today, isn't he?"

"Oh, he's gone to the hospital for a checkup. Pregnant men get far more checkups than women do."

"Shouldn't you have gone with him? Did you stay behind because of me? I'm sorry."

"It's fine. Saku says he's more comfortable going alone."

"Well, if you're sure . . ."

I dithered over which apartment I should take Juri to, but in the end we went to mine.

She looked put out to see the sofa bed there.

"Is this your bedroom? Are you sure you don't mind me coming in here?"

"Not at all. We use Saku's apartment as the bedroom, but I got the sofa bed so I can take naps in here when I want. Sorry it's so cramped."

"Oh, I don't mind that, but . . ."

I put some tea and cake on the small table and sat down to face her.

"It's quite tough getting out here, isn't it? Thanks for coming all this way to see me."

"I wanted to see you, so I don't mind. But the travel formalities *are* pretty strict."

"That's because it's still experimental. Once the experiment has succeeded, I think it will be easier for people to come and go."

"I do hope so. Visitors won't make the effort to come if it's this hard."

Juri sighed and fiddled with the rubber bracelet on her right wrist.

Nonresidents also had to first go to Narita in order to enter Chiba. They had to say how many days they would stay, and a bracelet equipped with GPS was placed on their wrist. If they exceeded the number of days, prefectural staff would come to remind them.

Juri had only come for the day, so she didn't have to go through too many checks, but it was stricter for people who were going to stay overnight. I knew the aim was to maintain the perfect, computer-managed population, so having people sneaking in and living there illegally would be a problem, but it made the entire city feel like a giant locked room.

Juri leafed through a pamphlet she was holding. The front cover read, "How about staying here permanently?" Once someone had completed the stringent checks and was finally allowed in, then they were invited to simply remain in Experiment City: "Submit an application form now and stay for good!" It was hardly surprising that visitors were bewildered.

Juri sighed and took a sip of tea. "I find this place kind of creepy. When you come out of the station, children are calling everyone Mother and crowding around them. They even called me Mother."

"Yes, I was taken aback by that at first too."

"When you moved here, you had to dissolve your marriage on paper, didn't you? But you're still a couple, aren't you? You really did elope, didn't you?"

Juri was convinced that we loved each other deeply, and seemed to be impressed by this.

"Once you have a child, bring it out of here and come back home to our world."

"Um, yes . . . I should talk it over with Saku," I said evasively and took a sip of tea.

Mizuto used to say that it must be lonely to live your whole life alone, and I'd agreed, but now that I was spending my days among other people all living the same way, I was beginning to feel that this was our original nature as animals.

Since everyone in this world was a Mother, you could easily buy adult goods for sexual relief at the convenience store. Basic gadgets and CDs of sexual fetishes were on sale alongside menstrual products, readily available for instant physical satisfaction. Love had nothing to do with this, and my Prada pouch containing my forty lovers was still shut away in the closet. I was busy showering the Kodomo-chans with affection and couldn't take time to enjoy sex, and I'd drifted toward more convenient methods. My lovers were still precious to me even now, but it was true that I tended to forget them once I'd disposed of my sexual needs.

I'd already started forgetting Mizuto despite not having found a new lover. I had been slowly adapting to this new world, which was apparently a more potent drug than love.

If I felt lonely, I could go to the park and children would snuggle up to me like pet animals and call me Mother. If I wanted to cuddle a baby, all I had to do was go to the Baby Room at the Center, where there would always be about twenty children, and staff members would show me how to pick them up, give them milk, and change their diapers.

Why had I ever wanted a family? There were times when I no longer knew the answer to this question.

The biggest motive had probably been loneliness, I thought. But here in this world everyone lived alone, and yet any sensation of loneliness had simply vanished.

I'd come to believe that the system we called "family" was just one of many systems animals had for breeding. Even if this Paradise-Eden system ultimately failed, we had at least discovered that there were many other possibilities.

The one tenuous link I still had with family was simply that I wanted to meet the child that had inherited my genes. But the more I thought about it, even this felt uncertain.

In reality, we're already lost, my husband had once said, and I couldn't get this out of my head.

Even in this world, *I was normal*. In all worlds, including the one my mother had given me and the world outside that one, and this Experiment City, I was so normal that it felt creepy. So much so that it was abnormal.

"This cake is delicious."

"Really? I'm so glad. I like it too."

"It's so sunny here and surrounded by nature, a really lovely place. If it wasn't for the fact that this is Experiment City, I might even want to live here."

"Why don't you move here?"

If she submitted the application form inserted into the pamphlet she'd received at Narita, she could stay right away. I waved the pamphlet on the table at her.

"No way," Juri said, showing her white teeth as she smiled.

For a moment her perfectly poised smile looked superimposed with a Kodomo-chan and I felt dizzy.

"Is something wrong?" She peered into my face with her big eyes. "You look pale. Ah, just as I thought. Life in this place doesn't actually suit you, does it?"

Her thick eyelashes looked like a leggy insect was sitting in the gap between her eyelids, and I stiffened.

When I didn't say anything, she tilted her head questioningly.

"Amane?"

Here and there on our bare white skin were holes through which organs were visible. We were creepy creatures with thick hair growing only on our heads. Was that what we looked like?

Juri opened her lips, revealing a squirming wet organ that emitted noise inside.

"You're being really weird, Amane. Maybe you should lie down?"

"Um . . . thanks. I'm okay."

"It was such a pity your pregnancy didn't work out this time. Of course you're tired. You should have a good rest, and don't rush things," Juri said gently.

Yes, this is what normal used to be in the world we were in until not long ago, I thought, relieved.

After my miscarriage, I'd had a new contraceptive device fitted at the hospital. My period and the ovulation I used to feel every month no longer hurt, and I didn't even get light bleeds anymore, just tiny amounts of a clear liquid excretion.

In the near future, maybe Juri's womb would excrete the same liquid and we would have totally forgotten all about the light bleeds that had once come from our bodies.

Outside the window was the pure-white town. It looked like countless nests, square chrysalises, stretching out as far as I could see.

"Well, here's to us!"

"It's been ages since we've been out together, just the two of us like this!"

"Yeah, it must be the first time we've been to a decent restaurant since we came to Chiba."

One day in June Saku and I decided to have dinner together. It was our wedding anniversary and it just happened to fall on a Friday, so we'd made a reservation at a classy restaurant by the station.

Since my husband was pregnant, we'd booked a private room so we could enjoy our meal in peace. The various courses were brought in and placed on the white tablecloth.

It had been some time since I'd last seen my husband, and his artificial womb was surprisingly swollen. It looked like the equivalent of a seven-month pregnancy in a woman.

"My belly's got so heavy that it's dragging down," he said, explaining that he was wearing a special maternity belt.

Now that the baby was getting big, I thought it must be rough going with the womb so exposed, but he looked happy.

"Amane, come here and have a look," he said after we'd finished the appetizer, so I got up and went over to where he was sitting. He rolled the maternity belt down so that I could see his bare womb.

I was dumbfounded. The shape of a child was visible, as though wrapped tightly in flesh-colored plastic wrap. It was so clearly defined that I could even see its movements with my own eyes.

"It's a boy. See?" He pointed at the womb, and sure enough, between the baby's legs, faintly visible, was what appeared to be a penis. "We pregnant men don't even need to have an ultrasound, do we? Look, he's smiling!" He fiddled happily with his belly.

I couldn't tell if the fetus was smiling or not. "Wouldn't it be better not to touch it too much?"

"It's okay, they told me this artificial womb absorbs all minor shocks or external stimuli. Science is amazing, isn't it?"

There was some stubble around my husband's mouth, and some of his soup had stuck to it. For a moment it looked like vomit, and just the thought that there must be more of the same liquid in his mouth made me feel like throwing up.

He must have been sweating, and the sweet smell of sweat mixed with soup wafted over to me.

I hung my head and, returning to my seat, concentrated on my own meal.

Since he was pregnant, my husband ordered a non-alcoholic cocktail, while I drank wine alone.

Suddenly my husband looked up with a grimace. "You're swilling the wine around in your mouth again, aren't you, Amane?"

"Huh? But that's how you're supposed to taste wine."

"Well yes, but the way you do it is different. It usually tastes best when you wash it back to your throat. And your way is gross."

I almost lost my temper, but instead I bit my tongue and finished my meal without drinking another drop of wine.

I wanted to get back to my nice clean room as quickly as possible. I wanted to eat what I liked, how I liked, and if I started feeling a sexual urge, I would dispose of it from my body quietly by myself. The sooner I got back to my clean room, the better.

During the meal, the waiter was extremely solicitous of my pregnant husband.

"Are you feeling cold? I can adjust the heating at any time, so please don't hesitate to tell me. And please use these to get comfortable," he said, bringing a blanket for his knees and a cushion to support his back.

When I thanked him, the waiter smiled as though it was no trouble at all.

"It's our Kodomo-chan, so it's only natural."

After we finished our meal and came out of the private room, the other customers in the restaurant called out, "Oh look, you're carrying our Kodomo-chan!"

"It's getting big, isn't it? Adorable."

"I can't wait until it's born!"

Everyone was looking at my husband's womb and smiling, all looking forward to their own Kodomo-chan coming out of it.

I desperately tried to convince myself that what was in there was my own egg, and that it was only *our* child.

That was all that was holding me and my husband together.

Hurry up and break out of my husband before we're completely assimilated into this world! I prayed silently with all my heart. I had the distinct feeling I could hear our baby wriggle inside my husband.

* * *

Near the end of June, we received notice of the landlord's passing.

Around this time, the whole town was brimming with women with huge bellies. It reminded me of the spawning sea turtles my husband and I had once seen on TV. We'd wondered why they had to give birth all at once, but now here we were, creatures engaging in the same behavior.

Very few men carried their baby through to the ninth month, but every now and then we saw a man with a large womb sac like my husband, both older and younger men.

At work we were insanely busy, with our general affairs manager, six female employees, and one man in sales pregnant and preparing to take maternity leave.

I was steadily losing contact with my husband. I knew that our baby was doing well only through text messages. He had told me that he would be admitted to the hospital at the end of the month, and I replied asking him to let me know the date once it was decided.

I was just thinking that when my husband went into the hospital I'd be busier than ever, when the news of the landlord's death arrived.

"What shall we do? We have to go to the funeral, right?"

The landlord had helped us so many times, even picking us up from the hospital after our insemination. Hearing that his funeral was tomorrow, I called my husband.

This world was completely centered around pregnancy, so this sudden intrusion of death felt strange.

"Yes, of course I'll go. Are my funeral clothes at your place?"

"Probably. They must be in a box. I'll take a look."

"Ah, but I won't fit into regular clothes. I'll have to look for pregnancy funeral wear."

Having discussed the matter on the phone, we arranged to meet the next day, and together we headed to the venue for the landlord's funeral.

The funeral wear he'd bought at the large supermarket by the station turned out to be a large black dress that covered his womb.

"I'm almost due, so this was the only thing that fit."

Dressed in mourning clothes that were exactly the same shape as the white smocks the Kodomo-chans wore, my husband looked like a stranger to me.

The funeral was held in a hall next to our apartment block. A group of children dressed in black was coming from the other direction, Kodomo-chans from the nearby Center who had come to attend the ceremony.

It had probably been judged inappropriate for the very youngest children to come to the funeral, so those attending were all from kindergarten to elementary age and able to walk by themselves.

People dressed formally in black were gathered in the funeral hall, and at first glance it looked as though the gathering would not be all that different from those in the other world.

There was an altar and folding chairs, and my husband and I sat next to each other toward the back, listening to the chanting of the sutras. Many of the Mothers we often saw in the park were there, both male and female, and of all ages. The landlord had enthusiastically attended the park and the Baby Room, so many of them were probably his friends.

The Kodomo-chans we'd seen on the way were lined up in the hall. Once the memorial address was over, the woman officiating the ceremony said, "Now we will read a letter of condolence from the Kodomo-chans to their Mother."

The eldest of them, around year four of elementary school, came to the front to read the letter.

Since they all had identical short, bobbed haircuts, I hadn't been able to tell, but from the voice it sounded like a boy.

The Kodomo-chan held its head high and briskly read the letter.

"Our dear Mother, thank you for everything you have done for us.

"We, our Mother's children, are cups for carrying life into the future.

"With our bodies we will carry the life we received from our Mother into the future. We will carry it faithfully into the future, taking care not to spill it, and some day, just like Mother, we too will become lovely Mothers, and pour our lives into the next cup.

"Thank you for everything."

There was a round of applause, and the Mothers all sniffled and dabbed the corners of their eyes with handkerchiefs.

The Kodomo-chans all shed tears. They all moved their facial muscles in exactly the same way when they cried, just like when they smiled. They all wept with slightly narrowed eyes, the muscles of their checks bulging slightly as they kept their lips shut and stretched to the sides as hard as they could. Drops of water flowed at the same speed down their cheeks.

Not a single child cried with its mouth open, or with one side of its face twisted.

The staff members with them also wept in the exact same way.

I was watching this, feeling queasy, when I heard the sound of sniffling next to me and saw my husband dabbing at his eyes with a handkerchief.

When it was our turn to go to the front to burn incense, I was taken aback to find that what I'd assumed was a coffin was actually a small wooden box containing the already cremated remains of the landlord.

And there were no bones left in the remains as there usually were. The landlord's bones had all been reduced to a beautiful white powder.

"Now we shall all go together to bury the remains," came the officiating woman's voice, and everyone filed outside. Following their lead, my husband and I were just through the exit when a man wearing a name badge from the funeral company handed us each a plastic cup.

Inside was a white powder. Realizing that it must be the landlord, I almost dropped the cup.

The man with the name badge put his hands around the cup to steady it, and in a cheerful voice said, "Please take care. Well then, shall we all carry Mother together?"

Cups in hand, all the people in mourning dress formed a black line and left the hall in a procession through the town.

The graveyard was behind the Center where the children lived. A square hole about the size of a swimming pool had been dug there and was being filled in with the white sand remains of all the people who had died in Experiment City.

"Everyone, please empty the cups in here. With your help, we shall put the Mother who has finished carrying life together with all the other Mothers who have died."

Silently, everyone added the powder in the cup to the white sand, put their hands together in prayer, and then walked away. My husband and I also poured out our cups of white powder.

The sandpit made from bones was faintly illuminated and was a beautiful brilliant white. The Mothers had become a single large mass that was steadily watching over us.

Would our bones one day be poured in here? Then we too would become part of the mass of all the Mothers.

This was such a strange sight, I thought, but part of me also somehow felt that this was how things had always been.

A new world was being imprinted in me. Like a newborn baby, I had absorbed everything in the world in front of me and had steadily become human. Even now I was still absorbing the world around me. And I was transforming into a person who took the shape of this world.

On the way back from the funeral, my husband dabbed at his eyes with his handkerchief and said, "I received life from Mother. I'll do my best to safely give birth to this baby and become a medium connecting life to the future."

"I guess."

"My admission date has been settled, you know. It's rare for a man to carry the pregnancy this far, so it seems they want me to go in a bit early. They're also putting me in a private room."

"Mm, I'll come and see you as often as I can. You'll need a change of clothes and other necessities, won't you?"

"Thank you, that would be a real help."

I looked around and saw a line of people in mourning clothes from the funeral walking behind us. Their black clothes were like small holes in the darkness. It was as though countless holes were slowly approaching us in the dark street.

When my husband was admitted to the hospital in August and I started visiting him daily, it hardly seemed possible that we'd barely met at all over the past few months.

My husband was one of only two men who had managed to carry a pregnancy in the artificial womb to full term. All extraneous visits and media interviews were stopped as the doctors and nurses focused on his care.

I was given a pass that allowed me access to my husband's room in the hospital, given that I was his close friend and next-door neighbor.

"I feel like a lab animal," he said self-deprecatingly, although he sounded a bit proud.

In fact, he *was* a lab animal, and that was why he was receiving such attentive treatment, but I didn't say so because I didn't want to upset his prenatal care.

When we could actually see the baby smile, my husband happily stroked the womb. He didn't look so much pregnant as possessed by a giant parasite.

"I'm getting a craving for sweet things. I guess the baby's asking for it. Especially anything with fresh cream," he would say, so I brought him some cake every day.

"Thank you, Amane."

"How are you feeling?"

"I feel great. So much so that I'm bored with not being allowed outside."

He zapped through TV channels while he ate his cake. "TV from the other world is so trashy, isn't it?" he said with a shrug. He had also started referring to anywhere outside Experiment City as the other world. "Don't you think so too, Amane? It's not as refined as our world here."

"Well, I don't watch TV much. By the way, it's almost time for your bath."

"Oh, is it that time already? I'm a bit sleepy."

"If it's too much of a burden on your body, there's no need to force yourself."

"No, I'll go. I have the feeling the baby wants to go too," he said, picking up his womb.

Helping my husband with his bath was part of my daily routine in the hospital. I washed his back and the womb with the baby inside. I had always avoided seeing him naked when we were married, but I was used to it now.

"Amane, look! The baby's smiling!" he said laughing, pointing at the baby now covered in soap bubbles.

Outside, the entire town was full of pregnant women. Many of the women hadn't gone into the hospital yet, and there were so many people with big, swollen bellies coming and going that the town looked as though it would explode with new life at any moment.

On my way home from the hospital, I dropped by the park to play with the Kodomo-chans. It was quite late and the park was crowded with Mothers on their way home from work, so I sat on a bench chatting with another Mother.

"There are a lot of male Mothers here today, aren't there?"

"There are. Equal numbers are inseminated, but as the pregnancies get closer to term, it's mostly women who are still pregnant, so the male Mothers stand out more in the park.

"Ah, I see."

"By the way, have you heard about the new Clean Room for adults they're installing by the station?"

"Clean Room?"

"Well, you see, when you become an adult, sexual urges build up in your body, right? It's the vestiges of copulation, but it's such a nuisance. So it's a bit like a toilet for eliminating sexual arousal and cleansing your body. Convenient, huh? Until now we've had to hide away in the privacy of our own homes to deal with it, but now we don't have to put up with this and can get rid of it right away."

So the world had shifted again, I thought. I didn't know how this Clean Room worked, but what we called masturbation was probably going to disappear from this world too. Part of me thought how convenient this would be. Our sexuality was evolving, and the world was continuing to adapt accordingly. Part of me accepted this.

"Things are getting more and more convenient, aren't they?"

"It's true. It's great to be living in the most advanced city."

The other Mothers were laughing. I too opened my mouth a little, to show my teeth, and made a cavity in my face to look like I was smiling. I had the feeling that the faces of the Mothers all smiling at once had exactly the same facial muscle movements as the Kodomo-chans they were with.

* * *

When I got home, I was relieved to be in my darkened apartment. Without turning on the lights, I lay down on the bed.

I switched on the TV just as the newscaster was solemnly explaining the new Clean Room.

> Clean Rooms are already in operation in Experiment Cities abroad and are at last going to be installed in Japan's Experiment City. The user goes into a private room and enters their personal data into a touch panel, and can then cleanse sexual arousal from their body faster than ever through the senses of sight, hearing, and smell, with electronic vibrations. Users also have the option to purchase a throw-away antibacterial device to dispose of your libido without wasting time, so it will be less troublesome than before. It takes about one to five minutes to cleanse the body, depending on the person.

Hearing this, I was prompted to open the drawer in my closet and look at the Prada pouch containing all my lovers. I was scared that they might have died after being left untouched at the back of the drawer for months now. I had loved them because they lived in the other world. That was true, but I had the feeling that like the landlord's bones, they had turned into white powder and become a single mass. I quietly closed the drawer without picking up the pouch. They would forever be lovers, not tools for dealing with my sexual urges. While I'd been so busy, I had fallen into the habit of saving time by only making use of the cheapest, most convenient tools to douse my sexual arousal as quickly as possible without the cumbersome association with the emotion of love.

I hadn't had a single new lover since coming to this town. Before coming here, I had felt lost without a lover, always being dragged around by my emotions.

I would probably never make love, even with nonreal people, again. Sexual arousal was no longer the sweet product of love but an excretion that kept building up in my lower belly, causing an unpleasant throbbing sensation.

The sexual urge that had been so precious to me now even felt trivial and intrusive. I disposed of the heat in my body and dozed in my clean room.

I was fitting into this world too well.

What kind of animals would we be, say, a thousand years from now? With these kinds of thoughts running through my mind, before I knew it I'd fallen asleep.

There wasn't a cloud in the sky on the day my husband gave birth.

As his designated companion, I had been given special permission to watch the delivery through the glass window of the operating room.

There was no opening in the artificial womb for the baby to come out of, so an incision would have to be made for the baby to be born by cesarean section.

My husband was lying on the bed. He was anesthetized but awake and looking anxiously at the ceiling.

I'd assumed I wouldn't be able to see the incision for the cesarean section from where I sat, but actually his entire body was visible. My husband's face was fixed in place so that he couldn't see his own operation. I had my face up close to the glass, watching intently on his behalf.

"Well then, shall we start?" the obstetrician said, and my husband's cesarean section began.

At a signal from the doctor, two nurses standing on either side of my husband's bed lifted up his womb. I could see the baby tossing and turning inside the sac.

Wearing gloves, the doctor used silver scissors to cut around the top of the sac as the nurses supported it. I knew there could be no sensation of pain with the artificial skin, but it looked painful nevertheless. Still, I kept watching the doctor making the incision without averting my eyes.

Blood started flowing out of the womb, as though a blood vessel had been cut.

"Just a little longer, hang on in there!"

My husband's face was pale, and I wondered anxiously whether he had somehow died. I wiped the sweat from my forehead.

Once the doctor had cut the top of the sac and made a hole, he proceeded to make a vertical incision. The womb turned inside out, revealing the inside of the artificial skin, where a pale fetus appeared, covered in my husband's blood and attached to plastic blood vessels and an artificial umbilical cord.

His face solemn, the doctor continued to make cuts in the sac until finally it gaped wide open and the crying baby was brought out.

"It's a success!"

The doctor held the blood-covered baby up as its cries rang out through the operating room.

We've become a different form of animal, I thought as I watched dumbfounded through the glass. The scene that had unfolded before my eyes was nothing like the way the animal I knew as human gave birth.

Covered with blood and wrinkled like a giant testicle, the baby was held up in the white operating room for all to see.

Beneath it lay my husband, his penis dangling alongside his womb. The womb now lay cut open, resembling a flower made of artificial meat in full bloom. My husband looked up at the baby with tears streaming down his face, the large sac-flower blooming on his belly.

The scene entered my retinas and seared itself into every last corner of my inner organs. I could feel all the cells in my body absorbing what I was seeing. Unfolding on the other side of the glass was a spectacle of absolute life. All the cells in my body trembled with excitement at the miraculous event of life coming into being right before my eyes. The emergence of a new life had forced strong emotions to well up in me.

A new Kodomo-chan belonging to all Mothers had come into being through my husband's body.

The doctor and nurses, too, were Mothers, and were all gazing happily upon the baby, cooing at it in sweet voices.

"Kodomo-chan, hey, I'm your Mother."

"I'm your Mother too."

"Look, you have another Mother over here too."

This was unmistakably a Kodomo-chan, identical to all the many other beloved Kodomo-chans, nothing more, nothing less. Its head was now covered in newborn fuzz, but it would eventually have its hair cut in a short bob and grow up exactly the same as the numerous Kodomo-chans I'd hugged in the park yesterday.

The bawling Kodomo-chan baby now had a face that resembled nobody else's, but its facial muscles would naturally take on the same movements as those of all the other Kodomo-chans. And it would come to smile, talk, and cry with the same facial expressions as all the many other Kodomo-chans.

I stared at the Kodomo-chan as though clinging to the baby that did not yet resemble anyone else. The Kodomo-chan's shrill voice sounded like the cries of an unknown animal I was seeing for the first time.

* * *

The following days passed in a blur. I was shooed out of the hospital and, unable to see my husband, spent my days endlessly watching the news broadcasts about the first successful birth from an artificial womb. It was two weeks after the birth of our child before I finally managed to contact my husband, who had been busy with both checkups and media interviews.

When I finally got permission to visit, I went to his hospital room with some flowers.

"How are you feeling?"

"Oh, the wound has already closed, and I just want to get out of here as soon as I can!"

"And the baby?"

"It's gone to the Center."

I held my breath. I'd already had the feeling for some time that this was how it would turn out.

"I see," I said quietly. "Is it okay? Once they go there, nobody can tell which one is which, can they? Will we be able to get our baby back?"

"I mean, isn't it better this way? Our children are all around us anyway."

He gazed out of the window. The children running around out there were all strangers.

There was no hope, I thought.

Both my husband and I had ingested too much of this world, and we had become normal people here.

Normality is the creepiest madness there is. This was all insane, yet it was so right.

Gazing fondly at the children playing outside the window, my husband said, "I'm happy. We have finally returned to paradise. We give birth to children and become Mothers to all children. We were getting it wrong all along, you and I. We couldn't bring ourselves to completely abandon the customs from the time when we couldn't have children without having sex. This place is the world we've been longing for all this time. Don't you think?"

I couldn't say anything.

"By giving birth, I've proved that artificial wombs can produce children. What an honor!" my husband said, enraptured. "Using my womb, I've given the world life. Don't you think that's wonderful?"

I hesitated a moment, then murmured vacantly, "I guess . . . but you promised me. We made a pact, you and I. We were going to bring up our child together . . ."

"We were wrong to think that way. Life belongs to all humanity, so we have to give it back to everyone." He shook his head wearily. "If you give birth yourself, Amane, you'll understand. There's no such thing as your 'own' child. However much you suffered through the pregnancy, the Kodomo-chan belongs to all humankind."

I couldn't find any more words to counter his reproving tone. "Well, I should be going then . . ."

"Yes, I've got to go for some more tests now. After all, I've become the first man to succeed in giving birth."

I walked out of the room, leaving my exultant husband behind. From far off I could faintly hear the cries of numerous newborn Kodomo-chans. The thought that all of them were my children welled up in me. A feeling was now sprouting in my body, completely different from the emotions and impulses I'd always believed were instinctive and physiological.

I wanted to test my own instinct. Spurred on by the impulse I'd forgotten since coming to Experiment City, I staggered along the white corridors of the hospital, longing to get closer to those voices.

"Mo-ther!" I heard someone call me. I looked out the hospital window and saw several Kodomo-chans heading off somewhere.

I had come to another part of the building, to a door labeled NEWBORN CENTER. I'd heard that all newborns were first brought here, and that the healthiest ones were selected to be taken to the Baby Room.

I wanted to see for myself what the Kodomo-chans lying in rows on the other side of this door looked like. I wanted to see if they were any different from the Kodomo-chan with my genes engraved in its body, the one that had been held up over my husband's head that day. I simply had to ascertain whether there was still any trace of the instinct that I had always believed was within me.

The door was locked and wouldn't budge an inch however much I pushed or pulled it.

"What do you think you're doing?"

Startled, I abruptly stopped what I was doing.

"You're not allowed in here. Which ward are you on?"

I timidly turned around and said hoarsely, "Um . . . Can I see the Kodomo-chans, even just for a moment?"

"It's not allowed. And even if you could see them, you wouldn't be able to tell which was the baby you gave birth to," the nurse said with a frown. She seemed to think that I was an inpatient who had just given birth and had come to find her own child.

"No, no, that's not it. I was inseminated last Christmas, but it . . . I just wanted to get a glimpse of the babies that were born safely," I explained.

Her expression softened. "I see. That must have been tough for you physically too . . . Well, okay then. I'll let you have a quick look inside. In fact, there was another Mother here this morning who had a stillbirth like you. She was reassured by just seeing the babies, that was enough to help her. I'm sure it will be the same for you too," she said, apparently mistaking me for a Mother who had just had a stillbirth.

The nurse took a keycard from her pocket and opened the door to the Newborn Center. I'd expected the babies to be right there, but the door opened up onto a long corridor that appeared to lead to a different building.

"We have a dedicated building where we care for all the babies born in this hospital," she said.

"Um . . . Do you mind if I ask you something strange?" I asked in a small voice, doing my best to keep up with her as she strode quickly down the corridor.

"What is it?" she answered amiably.

Somewhat reassured, I said, "Um, did you ever experience childbirth in the other world?"

"Yes, I did. Why are you asking?"

"Then why did you come to this world?"

She glanced at me and smiled. "I had a kind of premonition. This is the shape of our future."

I couldn't say anything.

She smiled at me gently. "I raised three children of my own there, you know. They were so, so cute. Cheeky and hard work, but very precious. I raised them believing that this was what motherhood was. But when I came here, I realized that, despite all the affection you feel for them, this instinct of going through the pain of childbirth and being dragged through life by your child only existed because it was convenient for society."

"Oh."

"But you know, the most important thing remains unchanged."

"What's that?"

"That is the healthiest thing for us human animals to do. Both mind and body follow the most important human purpose, which is to sustain life. In whatever form, I'm still a Mother. And so are you." She stopped before a large silver door. "The Kodomo-chans are in here. You can see them for just a moment, okay?"

"Yes."

The nurse inserted a different keycard and the silver door opened. "Please go in."

I took a deep breath and went through the door. The crying voices of babies rang out all around.

The facility was much bigger than I'd expected, with another corridor lined by glass windows on either side. I gulped and stared at the scene behind the glass. This was a giant field for growing humans. That was the only way I could describe it.

Rows of newborns stretched far into the distance behind the glass. I'd read somewhere that in the old days people talked about children being born in cabbage patches, and I thought it must have been a premonition of this scene.

Nurses in white uniforms were moving around this huge human field, giving milk to the babies.

"Um, shouldn't the babies have partitions between them?" I asked, concerned that there was nothing separating the rows of Kodomo-chans.

The nurse laughed. "What do you mean? They're all Kodomo-chans. They are each numbered with their own clinical record, but none of them has a name yet. The healthiest will be chosen and moved to the Baby Room. Of course, any sick babies receive treatment, but some do die."

I went up to the glass and gazed in again. To me, the pale cabbage patch babies looked just like swollen sperm.

My father's face in the photographs my mother had shown me when I was little came to mind. Had I been lined up like this in his testes just before being flushed into my mother? Just a submissively docile, unnamed, innocent, pure grain of existence that was a means to breed life?

I saw a few dead babies being carted away in the distance. Instantly some new children were brought in to fill the vacated spaces.

This cabbage field of life was no different from what I had been seeing in the world all along. The life grown here would eventually disappear, and life that was newly produced would be brought in. Grains of life would be brought in, and new life would fill the holes that had been made. This landscape of the cabbage patch would continue unchanged forever, with life being constantly replenished. We all were merely a display of life, nothing more. The world had always been that way. Life had always been what was right.

All of the Kodomo-chans here were mine. The child from my egg inseminated with my husband's sperm and born from my husband's womb was one and the same as all these rows of babies here.

I put my hand on the glass and smiled at my Kodomo-chans.

"Kodomo-chans, I'm your Mother. Look, Mother's here! Look over here!"

As if responding to my voice, several Kodomo-chans moved their eyes and started crying.

My life was in all of these children lined up here, uniformly, in equal amounts.

Was this my instinct now?

I felt like laughing out loud.

"Oh, what good timing," the nurse said, looking into the glass case. "Healthy Kodomo-chans are about to be taken into the Baby Room. Would you like to hold one?"

I nodded. The nurse opened a door onto what appeared to be the back entrance to the Newborn Center and called to a nurse transporting babies.

"Could I have a minute? This is a Mother whose Kodomo-chan was stillborn. Would you mind if she held one for a moment?"

The young nurse nodded and held a baby out to me. Wordlessly I took it in my arms.

"Oh, how cute!" I exclaimed, unable to contain my smile. "I wonder if my Kodomo-chan was as cute as this!"

"Of course. This one was born from your womb as well. All wombs are connected."

"I see, yes. My little Kodomo-chan. Hahaha, so cute! Hahaha! Hahahahahaha!"

I laughed out loud, and the Kodomo-chan smiled too, as if responding.

Men and women were now all the same, all wombs in service of the human race.

The inaudible music of rightness played over our heads, controlling us.

Before I knew it, that music was playing at top volume in my body. Obeying it, I kept calling sweetly to my own Kodomo-chan.

I couldn't help but be moved by the adorable, wriggling lives before my eyes. This was how the world let us know what was right.

We were, all of us, under the world's curse. Whatever form the world took, there was no escaping it. The newborn babies in rows before my eyes, the warm baby in my arms. The new life held up high, born in the blood shed by my husband. Faced with the obligatory rightness of the spectacle of connected life, unable to resist, we continued to obey it, moved by its wonders.

"It's so cute! It's so cute!"

"Our Kodomo-chans are all so cute, aren't they?"

"Cute! Cute! Cute! Cute! Cute! Cute!" we Mothers all said, and the Kodomo-chan in my arms smiled. It gazed upon the world with clear eyes, absorbing the world and becoming human, the same as me. Its entire body was being showered with the right world.

"Hahaha, this baby doesn't cry at all! Such a good Kodomo-chan!"

"Yes, and oh look, it has dimples. How cute! You really are such a cute Kodomo-chan!"

Several nurse Mothers all smiled and caressed our Kodomo-chan, speaking sweetly to it. The Kodomo-chan smiled at all its Mothers.

Beyond the glass was the huge field of tightly packed Kodomo-chans. All of those small, white, wriggling grains were my cute Kodomo-chans. I hugged the soft Kodomo-chan in my arms as though disgorging the affection welling up in me.

My mother came to visit from the other world, and fidgeted uncomfortably as I poured tea.

"This place is small, isn't it? Where's Saku?"

"Oh, he moved out. What can I say? He's the first man ever to successfully give birth. He's so busy that he's had to leave his job and now gives lectures and collaborates full-time with researchers at the hospital, apparently."

"Apparently? Don't you see him yourself?"

"No. We just exchanged a few things when he moved, but he was so busy that someone else came in his place. And I've been busy myself these days, giving milk to the new Kodomo-chans."

All the Kodomo-chans born around the same time were now almost one month old. We Mothers were going regularly to the Baby Room to help with their care, feeding them milk and cuddling them.

My mother frowned and exhaled disagreeably. "That's all the news anyone ever talks about out there too. I can't believe

Saku gave birth . . . I came because I was so worried, and look what I find . . ."

"He hasn't vacated his apartment yet, and I still have the key, so you can just move in, Mom. We can skip all the cumbersome paperwork."

"You've got to be joking," she spat out, scowling at me.

I couldn't help smiling at her. "How are things in the other world? Same as ever?"

"What do you mean, the other world?" Wrinkles appeared between her eyebrows.

I put a white plate with strawberry-and-cream sponge cake on it in front of her. "The Kodomo-chans made these plates at the neighborhood festival. Aren't they pretty?"

"Look, forget other people's children. What about your own child?"

"Ah, my own."

"Don't give me that! I came because I thought it must have been born by now and what do I find? Even if it didn't work out this year, there's always next year, isn't there? Talk things over properly with Saku. You're family, after all."

I laughed in spite of myself. Family. I hadn't heard that word for a while. It wasn't needed in this world.

"What are you laughing about? You're being weird," she said, grimacing.

I couldn't stop chuckling, and she glared at me.

"Don't you kind of think this way of life is okay too?" I asked her. "I get the feeling there's always a set number of people who don't really fit into society, whatever system is in place, and that percentage is always about the same."

"Huh?"

"Mom, whichever world you're in, around ten percent of the people there will always feel out of place, and you're among them. I'm one of those people who never feel out of place no matter where I am."

"There has always been that side to you, ever since you were little. You easily adapt to the ways of the world and get along just fine, at least on the surface. I can't do that. The instinct seared into my body from the beginning will never disappear. Never. It keeps burning within me."

"Right. That's the sort of person you are, Mom."

"But humans are not such convenient beings, you know. The data from the world you used to live in is still in there somewhere in your body. The data from the 'love and be loved and have children' world I stitched into your soul when you were a child is still in there. You can't escape from the instincts that were awoken in you in that world, you know. You were never without lovers in a world where sex was disappearing. That's the proof, more than anything else. I told you that I'd put a curse on you. Your instinct is to fall in love with someone and have children. That's what your instinct really longs for. I brought you up to live right."

I smiled and pointed at her empty cup. "Would you like some more tea?"

"Don't think you can fool me. There's no point putting on an innocent face like that. You know very well that thanks to me you've been brought up right."

"Haven't you ever thought that people are monsters?"

"Eh?"

"Not just people, but every living thing—all monsters. Even when we lived in the sea, we came out onto land, started flying through the sky, grew tails. We stood up on two feet, and started breeding through scientific means rather than animal copulation. Everything alive is a monster. I am too, and always have been."

For some reason my mother recoiled with a hurt expression, like a little girl.

"What's the matter? Would you like some cake?"

"You don't really mean that, do you? You're so easily influenced, you've just been brainwashed. Let's go home now. The other world is much better than this one."

"And you aren't brainwashed, Mom? Is there any such thing as a brain that hasn't been brainwashed? If anything, it's easier to go insane in the way best suited for your world."

My mother went pale and hung her head, keeping her eyes averted as though she thought I really was a monster.

"I'm leaving," she said, grabbing her bag. "If I carry on talking with you, I'll end up going crazy too."

"Okay. Would you like to take some cake with you?"

"No, thanks."

She tried to stand up but stumbled badly and fell off her chair, ending up on all fours on the floor.

"Ahhh . . ."

Her eyes were unfocused, maybe from the shock of being suddenly dizzy or perhaps drowsy as the sleeping pill took effect. She grasped desperately at the table, trying to get up, before falling back down on her knees, knocking the chair over.

"Mom, are you okay?" I wiped my lips with the paper napkin, stood up, and slowly went over to where she was kneeling.

"What did you . . . in the tea . . . ?"

"You see, Mom, I want to see the normal you."

"What the hell?"

"Whichever world I'm in, it drives me nuts to think I'm perfectly normal. Normal is the most terrifying madness in the world. Don't you agree?"

"Uhh." Unsteady and unable to talk properly, she glared at me fiercely.

"Mom, I'm scared. The power of normal takes over everything, takes me over even when I want to be abnormal. It keeps taking hold, and wherever I go I end up being a normal me."

She thrashed around on the floor as though drowning, opening and closing her mouth trying to speak.

"Look, Mom. You're the one who made me such a normal person. That's why I'm like this. Now it's your turn to become normal for me. It's time to go insane in this world, together with me."

She tried to crawl to the door, but the drug was too strong and she lay face down on the floor, twitching like a dying cockroach. Her flailing arms and legs gradually stopped moving as the drug took a deeper hold.

"I'm Mother's Kodomo-chan," I said, staring at her. "Isn't that so, Mother?"

Mother didn't answer. She must have fallen asleep.

Outside the window, the border between the clear sky and the pale-blue-and-white town blurred, and it felt as though I were floating up in the sky.

I could hear the laughing voices of the Kodomo-chans. Excited, shouting voices that tickled my eardrums, making them tremble.

Walking around the town on a cloudless day really did feel like living in the sky.

I was strolling along the light-blue promenade on my way home from work, thinking.

Here in the town our Kodomo-chans still looked exactly the same, no matter how many years had gone by. With their appearance unchanged even after several years, I myself was forgetting that I was getting older. I had now been inseminated several times, but I had not yet produced a Kodomo-chan with my own womb. But still, they were all around me in the town.

"Next time you're inseminated, you'll be able to choose whether to use your own womb or an artificial one," the doctor had told me last year when I turned thirty-nine, but I hadn't yet received a postcard notification.

I would go to the park after work whenever I didn't have any overtime, and on weekends I doted on the Kodomo-chans to my heart's content. By May, I started noticing men and women with swollen bellies around the town.

On my way home from work I always eliminated my sexual urge in the Clean Room outside the station. I preferred to do it there rather than at home, feeling that my apartment would be unsullied and cleaner that way. Cleansed, I headed to my own home.

There were Mothers who saw me as dirty for blithely using the Clean Room. I smiled at them. Even now, the world still continued to change. They and I were still evolving. We were just at different stages.

Since this town had been a success, there were apparently plans to start another Paradise-Eden in Kyushu. It was fun imagining it becoming a world every bit as beautiful as this one.

As usual, I eliminated my sexual desire at the Clean Room outside the station and stopped by the cafe next door for a takeout of my favorite coffee and headed for my apartment. It had become my custom to have some coffee and a rest before dinner.

I had just opened the automatic lock to my building and was going in when I saw a tall Kodomo-chan in a white smock struggling to put up a poster on the notice board in front of the apartment's mailboxes.

Hearing my footsteps, the Kodomo-chan turned happily to me. "Oh, hello Mother."

Some of the Kodomo-chans were bigger now than they'd been when I'd first moved here. The one before me now had long, slender arms and legs, and I could tell it was sweating by the beads of moisture on its pure-white paper-like skin.

"What are you doing?" I asked with a smile.

"I'm putting up a poster for the Mother's Day Festival at the Center," the Kodomo-chan said a little shyly. "We're making artificial carnations to give out to our Mothers. Please come too, Mother!" It spoke in a pleasantly brisk staccato, the way it had been taught.

"Of course I will. Are you going around all the apartments in this area? What a clever Kodomo-chan you are," I said, stroking its head.

"Don't treat me like a kid," it responded sulkily. "I'm not a Kodomo-chan anymore."

"You'll always be a Kodomo-chan to me. How's life in the Center? What have you eaten today? Don't you get lonely sometimes?" I asked casually.

The Kodomo-chan gave me a strange look, staring at me with its round, pitch-black eyes. "What does 'lonely' mean?"

Taken aback, I looked into the two marbles of its eyes. "'Lonely' means . . . um . . ."

Suddenly I couldn't remember what it had felt like to be lonely, and I tilted my head in confusion. I knew the word, but I couldn't remember the sensation. Maybe loneliness too was disappearing from my brain.

As I stood there smiling, my head still tilted, the Kodomo-chan came over to me with a look of concern and started rubbing my back.

"Mother, are you okay?"

Its arms were white, and it occurred to me that I didn't even know whether it was a boy or a girl. I turned to get a better look at its face, but I lost my balance and stumbled. Hot coffee splashed from the coffee cup I was holding in my hand, staining the Kodomo-chan's white smock.

"Ow!" it exclaimed in surprise, withdrawing its hand.

Flustered, I grabbed it. "Are you okay?" How could I have done such a thing to my own child?

"I'm okay, it's nothing."

"But it's hot! Did it burn you?"

"Um . . ."

"Come with me. You have to put it under water right away. You'll have to take your clothes off to stop it from burning more."

I ushered the Kodomo-chan into the elevator and hurriedly took it into my apartment, where I made it take off its white smock and undershirt while I ran cold water from the shower over the burn.

Its arm was a little red, but it didn't look serious, I thought with relief. I noticed that the Kodomo-chan didn't have breasts, so it was probably a boy.

"Thank you, Mother."

The sight of it meekly apologizing when I had burned it was so adorable, and I hugged it to me. "Sorry! I'm so sorry!" I said.

Having run cold water over the burn, I took out some black shorts and a sweatshirt from my drawer and handed them to the Kodomo-chan.

"Your pants got wet too, didn't they? I'll put them in the dryer now. These aren't your size, but don't worry about that."

"Okay. Thank you."

The Kodomo-chan smiled and without the slightest hesitation pulled down its pants and underwear in one go just as I was closing the bathroom door. Shocked, I stiffened.

"Is it okay to put these on without underpants?"

Seeing the child smiling and tilting his head, I realized that he didn't feel embarrassed in the least.

Stark naked, he looked up at me strangely. "Mother?"

"Ah . . ."

The Kodomo-chan's silky black bobbed hair swayed. I couldn't tell whether this was the same Kodomo-chan I had helped with its studies in the park yesterday, or the Kodomo-chan who had helped me with my heavy bag yesterday, or whether I had never seen those round eyes before.

With the same movements as countless other Kodomo-chans, he moved his eyelids, raised the muscles of his cheeks, and made his lips into the shape of a smile.

"Kodomo-chan . . ."

"What, Mother?"

"What would you do if I asked you if I could put this inside my body?" I asked, touching his small penis with my index finger. I wanted to know how much he was aware of his sex, whether he had any shyness about it at all.

The Kodomo-chan looked a little mystified, then smiled innocently, his teeth showing.

"I understand. Yes, originally we were all inside Mother's body, weren't we?"

The naked, smiling Kodomo-chan looked exactly like the picture of Adam in Eden that I'd seen once in a picture book. Outside Eden, what sort of sex had Adam and Eve had?

It was light inside the room, and we were both naked. Neither of us was the least bit embarrassed.

On the white sheets, I was *making* sex. I had to make it. I had forgotten how I used to do it, and sex had vanished from my body altogether.

I tried to do it by listening to the voice in my body, the way I'd done in the past, but quickly gave up. I no longer heard any voice coming from within me. I had knowledge, but it was like sex itself had been completely eliminated from my body. Maybe I—or humankind—had used it all up in the other world.

Uncertainly, I slotted the thing resembling a discarded snakeskin between the Kodomo-chan's legs into my body as if completing a puzzle.

My body remained quiet, with no brain excretions welling up. Maybe my body was no longer set up that way.

The Kodomo-chan's protrusion was beginning to harden, like dried paper clay.

The Kodomo-chan's mucous membranes induced a feeling of nostalgia in me. I had the sensation I was slowly remembering what it was like living surrounded by organs during the time I'd been in the womb.

I felt relief, and with that safe feeling, the mucous membranes throughout my body began to become wet, as though they were drooling. My eyes moistened, my nose began to drip, and water started to flow from my vagina too. I looked at the Kodomo-chan and saw it was the same with him. Maybe people were designed to discharge moisture when they felt safe.

My wet mucous membranes and the Kodomo-chan's wet mucous membranes came together trembling, like plants during pollination. The Kodomo-chan's protuberance was like a sticky pistil, and as I rubbed it, it produced bodily fluids and settled into my body.

There was no pleasure in this, just an almost mysterious sense of safety. Our muscles were relaxed, and we felt no pain at all.

As the Kodomo-chan's pistil-like protuberance was drawn into my body, he looked at me curiously.

"What are you doing, Mother?"

"You see, I'm making something. I'm trying to make something with my own body that nobody has ever made before."

"Wow, that's great, Mother. Amazing!"

His eyes shining, the Kodomo-chan stared at the pale protuberance that was connecting us.

All of a sudden, we heard someone pounding fiercely on the wall next door, in number 705.

She must have sensed that there was someone here in this apartment. The wall was shaking so hard that a picture I had up on the wall looked like it was about to fall off. Intermittently we heard something like an animal's howl.

"I wonder what that noise is," the Kodomo-chan said, staring at the wall.

I gently stroked his hair. "The apartment next door is empty, but I'm borrowing it at the moment. Look," I said, showing him the key I kept by the pillow.

The Kodomo-chan looked up at me curiously. "Is there something in there?"

"Yes, there is. I have a pet. She must be a little hungry. It's okay, I'll go feed her in a while."

"Wow, what kind of pet do you have?"

"Oh, she's super cute! She cries a lot, and she eats a lot."

The noise level went up a notch as we heard a chair being overturned. But after that, she must have given up, since things grew quiet again.

"Maybe she went to sleep. What do you feed her?"

"She eats all kinds of things, but what she likes best to consume is the world. She eats the world, and she becomes exactly like it. She's a really strange animal, but very interesting."

"Wow, incredible."

Moving our facial muscles in exactly the same way, the Kodomo-chan and I both lifted our cheeks, stretched our lips wide, and laughed showing the cavity between our teeth.

More water than ever before flowed from my body. Water poured out of the Kodomo-chan too, and drool flowed from his mouth as though a screw had come loose in him.

We were coiled together like plants after being watered.

Between us the Kodomo-chan's protuberance connected the two of us like a short, fat umbilical cord.

The umbilical cord extended from my vagina, connecting me to my Kodomo-chan. I reached a hand out to my Kodomo-chan, and our wet hands entwined. His laugh in that moment sounded just like the cry of a newborn baby.

Another loud groan came from the apartment next door. I listened to it fondly, thinking nostalgically that it must be the kind of sound that humans had made back when we were still animals. We had probably moaned like that when we used to copulate on all fours.

The human cry continued on and on. I no longer knew whether it was coming from next door or whether I was emitting it myself as I stroked the soft skin of the Kodomo-chan finally attached to my womb.